funny
kid

ABC
BOOKS

ykid

kicks butt

**written and illustrated
by Matt Stanton**

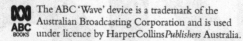
The ABC 'Wave' device is a trademark of the
Australian Broadcasting Corporation and is used
under licence by HarperCollins*Publishers* Australia.

First published in Australia in 2019
by HarperCollins*Children'sBooks*
a division of HarperCollins*Publishers* Australia Pty Limited
ABN 36 009 913 517
harpercollins.com.au

HarperCollins*Publishers*
Level 13, 201 Elizabeth Street, Sydney NSW 2000, Australia
Unit D1, 63 Apollo Drive, Rosedale, Auckland 0632, New Zealand
A 53, Sector 57, Noida, UP, India
1 London Bridge Street, London SE1 9GF, United Kingdom
2 Bloor Street East, 20th floor, Toronto, Ontario M4W 1A8, Canada
195 Broadway, New York NY 10007, USA

A catalogue record for this book is available
from the National Library of Australia

ISBN 978 0 7333 3602 7 (paperback)
ISBN 978 1 4607 0765 4 (ebook)

Cover and internal design by Matt Stanton
Typeset in Adobe Garamond by Kelli Lonergan
Author photograph by Jennifer Blau
Printed and bound in Australia by McPherson's Printing Group
The papers used by HarperCollins in the manufacture of this book are a
natural, recyclable product made from wood grown in sustainable plantation
forests. The fibre source and manufacturing processes meet recognised
international environmental standards, and carry certification.

To Levi, August and Rufus:
three of my favourite
superheroes.

1 Something's fishy.

A long, long, long time ago ... (Well, this morning.)

In a galaxy far, far, far away ... (Just around the corner, actually. At Hugo's place. He lives in an apartment block called Palm Grove. I always find that name funny because there's only one palm tree. A dead one.)

Duh! Duh-da-da-duh! Duh-DUH-da-da-duh-da-da-DUUUUHHHH!

(Wow, this orchestra sounds amazing! This must be what it's like to be a character in an action movie. I'm running around, chasing bad guys, fighting aliens, eating donuts and the whole time there's this big exciting music in the background and …)

'Hello?'

What? Who said that?

'Yes, speaking.'

And what happened to the music?

'No, I didn't order any dumplings.'

Huh?

'I think you have the wrong number.'

That's when I realise Hugo's mum is standing right behind me talking on her phone. The music was her ringtone. Turns out I'm the kind of character in the action movie who runs around, chases bad guys, fights aliens, eats donuts and gets his friend's mum to stand behind him playing music out of her phone.

Although I think I'm missing the point here.

The point is there are dumplings going around that no one seems to be claiming! I love dumplings! Send the dumplings over –

Hugo's mum hangs up.

Ugh. Okay. Fine.

Now, where were we? Oh, yes, Hugo and I are playing Captain Kickbutt. I am, of course, Captain Kickbutt: Intergalactic Security Force Agent 12, now with night-vision goggles, gamma-ray bazooka and utility belt. Batteries not included.

Hugo is my assistant, Norman.

Please note that I said 'assistant' and not 'sidekick'. Norman is not a sidekick. Captain Kickbutt does not need a sidekick. Norman was living a boring life as a scientist. Captain Kickbutt felt sorry for him, so he helped

Norman out by letting him make cool gadgets and vehicles for him, like the Kickbuttmobile with central locking and driver's side airbags (figurines sold separately).

Norman makes whatever Captain Kickbutt needs – like a ray gun or a grappling hook or a seven-cheese pizza. His famous catchphrase is: 'How can I be of service, Captain Kickbutt?' Hugo loves being Norman.

I HATE BEING NORMAN.

'But you're so good at it, Hugo,' I reply. 'Now, come on. I have to defeat the evil merman, Hammerhead.'

Hugo sighs. 'How can I be of service, Captain Kickbutt?'

Frankly, I think he could be a bit more enthusiastic.

FLIPPERS! I NEED FLIPPERS!

I run out of Hugo's front door and into the stairwell of the apartment block.

'I don't have any –'

I'm sure you know this already, but Captain Kickbutt is the greatest superhero of our time. His famous catchphrase is: 'I am Captain Kickbutt and I'm gonna kick your butt,' which he says in a deep, gravelly voice. It's a much cooler catchphrase than Norman's.

Captain Kickbutt has a jetpack, which is awesome. And as if that's not enough, in the latest season of the cartoon he upgraded it to the Sonic4000 model with air intakes and a hybrid engine, so now he can basically fly as fast as a fighter jet with a greatly reduced carbon footprint. He has wrist guards that shoot lasers, an indestructible shield that he can also sky-surf on, and the best hair of all time, which never gets blown out of shape in the wind! He saves the world pretty much every day and he's smashed more mutants and aliens than I've eaten cheeseballs … I think. I should probably check that. I've eaten a lot of cheeseballs.

For right now though: I am Captain Kickbutt and I'm gonna kick your butt!

I bump into Mrs Schmidt in the stairwell. She's Hugo's neighbour. I don't mean I just see her as she walks by. I mean I actually bump into her. She's on her bottom now.

'Oops! Sorry, Mrs Schmidt!' I call back over my shoulder. 'Norman! Can you help Mrs Schmidt?'

I run out of the apartment block, where I come face to face with Captain Kickbutt's arch-nemesis, Hammerhead (in this case, played by Bubbles the goldfish, whose bowl we put outside earlier).

The other day Mum asked me why I like Captain Kickbutt so much. She wondered if it was the costumes and the colours. She suggested that perhaps it was the fact that I got something called endorphins when I was running and jumping around. (I explained that Hammerhead's endolphin army doesn't come in until series two.) She hoped that it was Captain Kickbutt's pursuit of justice, his desire for peace, his commitment to defending the defenceless. I told her it was mostly just that Captain Kickbutt got to thump people and still be a good guy.

Norman comes running out. 'Max! We need to go!'

'Who's Max? My name is –'

'Max, it's time for your audition!'

Norman, it turns out, is also quite good at managing my schedule.

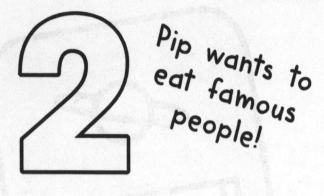

2 Pip wants to eat famous people!

So I have some news.

Wait for it.

All right. Here we go …

They are filming some scenes for the new *Captain Kickbutt* movie in Redhill.

Yes, you read that right. Here. In Redhill. Where I live.

Nothing ever happens in Redhill! This is probably the most incredible thing to happen since Bertha from the bakery won the lottery. She bought herself a jet-powered pogo stick and was never seen again. That was when I was three. The only other thing worth mentioning was the time the circus visited Redhill and an elephant got loose and knocked over a line of Portaloos. Can you imagine? You're sitting down to do your business when suddenly the entire toilet tips over with you inside. Actually … maybe don't imagine that too much. I heard some people got quite sick. It made the national news.

Anyway, none of this is important. What *is* important is that Pip and Tyson's dad is the famous actor George Khan. You've probably heard of him.

PIP

TYSON

GEORGE KHAN (famous actor)

He's playing Hammerhead in the new movie, which is great because there are probably going to be action figures of Pip and Tyson's dad in the toyshop. I can't imagine them making action figures of my dad. What would his weapon be? A spatula? I guess he could use his dressing gown as a cape.

Apparently there are going to be some scenes in the movie about Captain Kickbutt's childhood. Captain Kickbutt grew up in a place a bit like Redhill, so they're filming the kid scenes here. They've turned an old warehouse on the other side of town (which, rumour has it, used to store half the country's canned chicken soup) into a film studio where they've built a fake school. Redhill has gone Hollywood!

It gets even better than that. They're auditioning local talent to be in the movie, and if there's one thing I am, it's local talent. I'm the funny kid! And I think young Captain Kickbutt would have been a funny kid too. So who else do you think should get to play –

'Is he here yet?' Pip asks, looking everywhere. 'Is he here yet?'

See? Pip knows what I'm talking about. I cough when I walk up behind her.

'Who are you calling dinkle-squat?' I say. 'I'm about to be the star of the new *Captain Kickbutt* movie!'

I'm here at the film studio to audition. They're doing a casting call for kids who want to be in the movie. None of my friends want to be in it. They don't want to be famous. What they want is to *see* someone famous. I feel like they take me for granted.

CAPTAIN KICKBUTT HAS MUSCLES, MAX.

I HAVE MUSCLES.

I'd better show her. I flex. Hmmm, yeah. That's not really working. I'll show her later.

'And a pearly white grin,' says Pip.

'I also have a pearly white grin,' I reply and do my best celebrity smile.

Abby stares at me. 'And he's about six foot three.'

I'M ABOUT ... HEY, WELL, I'M GROWING, ALL RIGHT! ANYWAY, IT'S YOUNG CAPTAIN KICKBUTT THEY'RE FILMING IN REDHILL. HE WASN'T SIX FOOT THREE WHEN HE WAS A KID!

'But, Max, your name is not Spencer Daniels,' Pip sighs with a smile. 'And Spencer Daniels is the cutest thing on two legs.'

Oh, yeah. I forgot to mention him.

So there's a slight complication in my plan to be cast as the young Captain Kickbutt. It's just a little thing. They've actually *already* cast a young Captain Kickbutt. It's this Spencer Daniels kid who was on some TV talent show and the whole world decided was adorable. The little punk didn't even win. He was beaten by a very flexible singing acrobat. I'm sure, once I get into my audition, they'll realise that they've cast the wrong kid.

'Oh, yeah, him,' I say. 'I think he's my co-star.'

'Max, you're auditioning to be an extra,' Abby says. 'You're not the star of the movie.'

'Shhh,' I tell her, pulling a piece of paper out of my pocket. 'I'm practising my lines.'

'You're not going to have any –' Abby starts to say, but she gets interrupted by Tyson screaming like an excited goat.

'He's here!'

Sure enough, a car pulls up to the front of the studio and out gets Spencer Daniels.

Now, I won't admit this to the others, but I did do some googling of this kid earlier. He's eleven, just like me. He's regarded by most celebrity magazines as 'The Cutest', so that's a little bit like me, and he also seems to be good at practically everything ... so, bingo!

'The Cutest' gets out of a black limousine followed by an enormous muscly guy who must be his bodyguard. Spencer's mum climbs out next, carrying a small mountain of shopping bags. Mrs Daniels is also quite famous after crying like crazy on the TV talent show when her son sang an Italian opera. Everyone remembers because she was wearing a T-shirt that said, 'Spencer is a little god.'

'Oh, wow,' Pip gasps. 'It's really him! He's just so ... delicious.'

'Ew. Weird,' I say. Pip's a cannibal. Who knew? 'Now, where was I? I am Captain Kickbutt and I'm gonna kick your butt. I am Captain Kickbutt and I'm gonna kick your butt.'

'Pssst, Max,' Abby whispers. 'I hate to break it to you, but you're not going to be Captain Kickbutt. He is.'

YOU THINK I CAN'T HANDLE A LITTLE COMPETITION FROM SPENCER DANIELS? ONCE THEY SEE THAT I CAN ACT AS WELL AS MR TOOTHY-CUTIE-FACE OVER THERE, THEN MAYBE THEY'LL GET ME TO DO SOME REALLY COOL STUFF IN THE MOVIE. PLUS, I'M FUNNY. SPENCER DANIELS IS NOT FUNNY.

'Ooh.' Abby grins. 'So it's like Funny Kid versus Famous Kid.'

'Funny always wins.'

'I don't even know why you like this character anyway. He's such a boofhead. Have you ever read my Hailey Plum books? You should read my Hailey Plum books. They're so much better.' I realise Abby is holding one in her hand.

'Ooh, they sound interesting,' Hugo says. 'Can I borrow one?'

UGH. NO, HUGO. WHY WOULD YOU READ ABOUT HAILEY FRUITY-FACE WHEN THERE ARE SO MANY *CAPTAIN KICKBUTT* COMICS TO READ? IN THE NEW ONE THAT COMES OUT NEXT THURSDAY, HE'S GOING TO FIGHT EMPEROR POPSICLE WITH A BREADSTICK SOAKED IN LIQUID NITROGEN. I READ ABOUT IT ONLINE.

'That is SO dumb,' Abby says, rolling her eyes. 'That's what I love about Hailey Plum mysteries. She uses deductive reasoning and her superior observation skills to solve crimes. She's super clever.'

I do an enormous fake yawn. Which makes me really yawn. Which makes the first yawn look very obviously fake. I hate it when that happens.

'Oh, I'm sorry,' I say. 'I fell asleep. What were you saying?'

Abby Purcell glares at me.

That's when someone calls, 'Max Walburt? Has anyone seen Max Walburt?'

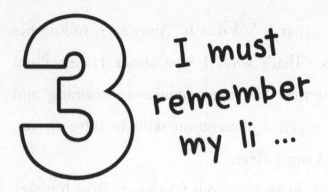

3 I must remember my li ...

'Come this way, please.'

The owner of the voice is a teeny tiny adult. He wears a tie, carries a clipboard and his poking nose and chirpy voice remind me of a parakeet.

It's audition time and I am prepared. I've written my script down on the piece of paper in my hand. It's only one sentence, really.

'I am Captain Kickbutt and I'm gonna kick your butt,' I whisper to myself. 'I am Captain Kickbutt and I'm gonna kick your butt.'

Apparently Parakeet thinks I'm talking to him.

TRY TO KICK MY BUTT AND I'LL FLY KICK YOU TO THE MOON, BUDDY.

'Oh, I didn't mean you –'

'Yeah, you'd better not have meant me,' Parakeet says. 'I know kung fu.'

He opens the door to the audition room and I step inside.

It's quite a big room and there's a table with four chairs along one side. Three are occupied and one is empty. The woman sitting in the middle is clearly the most important. She's wearing sunglasses inside. Only important people do that.

The two people either side of her lean back in their chairs and look like they're ready to sprint off and do jobs for her at a moment's notice. Parakeet sits down in the fourth chair.

YOU'RE MAX WALBURT?

She reads my name off a piece of paper. I don't need to read her name off a piece of paper though. I know exactly who she is. She's the director.

'And you're Rhonda Anderson Delaney,' I reply. 'I googled you.'

'Did you now?' the director says, rubbing her eyes under her glasses.

'You have three names,' I continue, 'and your initials are RAD.'

'Thanks for pointing that out,' Rhonda Anderson Delaney replies. I think she's appreciating the chit-chat, so I decide to keep talking.

'It's a good thing you went with the three names thing. Because RD ... that's just short for road. Not as cool.'

'Thanks for that, Max. That's my aim in life. To avoid being a road.' The director straightens her glasses and looks me up and down. It doesn't take her long. I'm not very tall. 'Now, are you ready to do some acting for us?'

'Of course,' I say, stuffing the piece of paper in my back pocket. I should be able to do it off by heart by now. 'I can do all of Captain Kickbutt's lines.'

'That's wonderful, but –'

Talking to adults is not always as difficult as it looks. You just have to start and then, whatever happens, keep talking. Believe it or not, adults seem to have a hard time interrupting kids, especially if you don't stop for a breath.

'Like: I am Captain Kickbutt and I'm gonna kick your butt,' I say. Oh, no, that was horrible. What happened? I have done it so much better than that before. It wasn't as low as it should be. I didn't put enough of a gravel sound in there.

'That's excellent, but –'

'Wait!' I say before she can kick me out, which I'm sure is what she was about to do. 'I can do it better.'

I take a deep breath and focus. Here we go:

Nailed it.

The director seems distracted. I imagine having to babysit that Spencer Daniels kid really takes it out of you.

'Actually, what I'd prefer you to do –' she starts to say, but then I realise she doesn't know that I've worked out exactly the best way to do the Captain Kickbutt voice. I'm probably the best at it in the world and I'm only eleven. It's all about technique.

I FIND THE BEST THING TO DO IS PRETEND THAT YOU'RE TRYING TO COUGH UP A BIT OF PHLEGM WHEN YOU TALK. I KNOW YOU WANT THAT SPENCER DANIELS TWERP TO BE CAPTAIN KICKBUTT, BUT DOES HE KNOW HOW TO DO IT PROPERLY? I GUESS I COULD SHOW HIM IF HE HASN'T QUITE GOT IT YET, BUT IT MIGHT BE EASIER JUST TO CAST ME AS CAPTAIN KICKBUTT INSTEAD, BECAUSE IT'S QUITE AN ART. IT'S EVEN BETTER IF YOU DO HAVE A BIT OF ACTUAL PHLEGM. MAYBE HE SHOULD TRY TO CATCH A COLD. LAYLA AT MY SCHOOL HAS A COLD AT THE MOMENT. MAYBE HE SHOULD HANG OUT WITH HER?

MAX!

See, I told you adults have a hard time interrupting kids. She takes a deep breath.

I JUST NEED SOME FACIAL EXPRESSIONS. CAN WE DO THAT?

'Oh, sure,' I say.

That's a little disappointing. Facial expressions? I feel like she's not really letting me reach my full potential here. I might need to take back control of this audition. She needs to see me at my best.

'I also do my own stunts though. Did I mention that? I wrote it on my application form.'

The director puts her head in her hands and I hear her whisper something like, 'This is why you should never work with children,' to the guy sitting next to her. I ignore that. She didn't mean it. Everyone likes working with children. Why else would you become a teacher? Or a babysitter? Or a prison guard in a kids' jail. However, she'd better pay attention, because I'm about to give her gold right here.

SEE, I WAS THINKING, WHEN YOU WANT AN ACTOR TO LOOK LIKE THEY'RE GETTING HURT, THEN YOU NEED TO USE A STUNT PERSON WHO JUST PRETENDS TO GET HURT. BUT WOULDN'T IT BE BETTER IF THE ACTOR WAS JUST WILLING TO GET HURT? I WOULD DO THAT FOR YOU. LIKE, IF YOU WANTED ME TO LOOK LIKE I WAS GOING TO RUN INTO THAT WALL, I WOULD ACTUALLY JUST RUN INTO THAT WALL.

'Max, that's great, but –'

'You don't believe me, do you? I understand. I'll show you.'

That's when I run into the wall. I run straight into it. No hands up to protect myself or anything.

My legs seem to be shocked that I actually did it, because they just decide to stop holding me up. I start to fall over. Out of the corner of my eye, I see the director leap to her feet.

'Max! Are you all right? What did you do that for?' she calls out.

'I'm fine,' I reply, watching the room spin around and around and around. Walls are really hard.

'Oh, for the love of … your parents are gonna sue me.' Rhonda Anderson Delaney comes running over.

'I'm sorry,' I say dreamily, and she tries to help me sit up. Woah. I'm feeling a bit sick. 'I'm just very excited.'

'I think he has a concussion. Look at his eyes,' Parakeet says.

'Get First Aid in here!' someone else calls out.

'I just really love Captain Kickbutt …' I moan, '… with my whole heart.'

'Shhh. Max, stop talking,' the director says. 'It's all right. You can come back on Monday afternoon.'

'I got it?' I ask.

'Sure. Whatever,' the director mutters.

Woohoo!

I can pass out now.

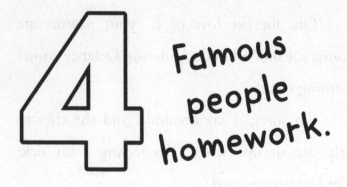

4 Famous people homework.

Sometimes to be extraordinary you have to do something extraordinary – like knock yourself mostly unconscious in an audition. It may not have been the plan and I'm not sure I would recommend it, but it worked and by eight o'clock the next morning my head has nearly stopped throbbing!

The end justifies the headache ... or something like that.

Hugo, Tyson and I are at the newsagent's, doing research on how to be a celebrity. I'm looking at some guy in a magazine called *SLICK* who has really crazy hair. How does he get it to stand up like that?

THINGS ARE GOING TO HAVE TO CHANGE AROUND HERE NOW THAT I'M GOING TO STAR IN THE *CAPTAIN KICKBUTT* MOVIE.

'Is that really what they said? That you're going to be Captain Kickbutt instead of Famous Kid?' Tyson asks. 'Because I spoke to my dad and –'

'Shhh!' I stop him. 'You weren't there, Tyson. They loved me. That's all there is to it. And now that I'm going to be a celebrity, I need to live like one. That means you two need to be my entourage.'

'Your what?' Hugo asks.

'It's called an entourage. All the famous people have them. Look.' I point to the pages of the magazine I'm holding. 'Famous people never go anywhere by themselves. There are always people walking around with them.'

JUST FOLLOWING THEM?

Tyson taps the photos in his magazine.

'Good point. We need to get one of those,' I say. 'Hugo, I'll leave that with you.'

'Are you going to do this too?' Hugo asks. 'This woman is carrying a puppy in her handbag.'

I think for a minute. I'm not really into animals. Except for my duck.

I have a pet duck called Duck. He's waiting outside the newsagent's for us because apparently you're not allowed to bring waterfowl inside. That'll change once they realise who I am.

'There's a girl down the street with a guinea pig,' I say. 'Maybe I could borrow that?'

We flick through a few more pages. Research is actually quite fun. I don't know why school tries so hard to make it boring.

'All these magazines keep talking about style,' Hugo notices. He points to a picture of some guy in a black jacket and pink pants. 'What is "style"?'

'I think it's something you buy online,' I say.

'No, no. My dad has some of it,' Tyson says. 'I think it's got to do with how you point your chin. Can you point your chin, Max?'

I DON'T REALLY HAVE A CHIN.

'That might be a problem.' Hugo screws up his face and points at all the chins in the magazine. There are a lot of chins. How am I supposed to get a chin?

'I'm going to be your bodyguard,' Tyson announces. 'Look at this.'

He flicks through the pages pointing to all the enormous muscly men and women standing out of focus and a bit behind the famous people.

Now that he points them out, they're everywhere.

'That would help to keep the crowds of people off me,' I admit.

'Yeah. It is. That's what his mum named him when he was born, I think.' Tyson nods. 'He's awesome. Dad's going to get me his autograph. I want to be just like him. So I'll be your bodyguard, Max. Don't worry, I'll keep the screaming girls away from you.'

'Thanks,' I say. 'It is important to have personal space.'

Suddenly, people outside the newsagent's start running and yelling. What's going on out there? Maybe there's a sale on at the gardening store again. I'm always amazed at how excited people can get about buying cheap cow poo.

Only that's not what's going on.

'The Goldsteins have been robbed!' someone calls into the newsagent's as they run by.

The Goldsteins? There's only one Goldstein family in Redhill that I know of. I turn to Hugo.

'Hugo, is that your parents' shop?'

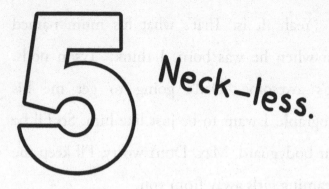

5 Neck-less.

Hugo's parents run a jewellery store in Redhill. It's called Goldstein's Jewellery. That's because it sells jewellery and their last name is Goldstein. I shouldn't have to explain all this. I would have thought it was pretty obvious.

Anyway, I don't know anything about jewellery except that girls and pirates seem to love it. Which is strange when you think about it, because not that many girls like pirates and not that many pirates like girls and yet they have so much in common!

My entourage and I run out of the newsagent's and head a few shops down to the jewellery store. There's a big crowd standing out the front already. Apparently everyone in Redhill has heard the news about the robbery except for us. And we were standing in a *news*agent's!

Even Abby and Pip are standing around watching.

HOW COME YOU GUYS ARE HERE?

I WAS PLAYING AT ABBY'S AND THEN HER MUM HAD TO COME DOWN HERE BECAUSE SHE'S THE DETECTIVE.

Abby's mum is Sergeant Purcell, one of the local police officers.

We look at the shop. The front window has been smashed! There's glass all over the ground and police tape has been put up to block off the crime scene. Sergeant Purcell is near the front of the store talking to Hugo's parents.

'Mum? Dad?' Hugo calls out as he pushes through the crowd of people. 'What happened?'

Mr Goldstein comes over to us.

NOTHING TO WORRY ABOUT, HUGO. NO ONE'S BEEN HURT. WE'VE BEEN ROBBED THOUGH. SOMEONE STOLE A NECKLACE.

THEY SMASHED THE WINDOW AND BROKE IN?

Hugo goes inside with his mum and dad and the rest of us stand around and watch the drama. Above the smashed window is the flashing blue light of the security alarm. Sitting on the carpet inside is a brick, which someone must have thrown to smash the window. Poor Mr and Mrs Goldstein. Who would do something like this?

'Tell me, Max,' Abby says. 'What do you think Captain Kickbutt would do in this situation?'

'That's easy,' I say. 'He'd catch the bad guys.'

'Yeah, but how?'

'He'd … I dunno. I guess he would … well …'

Abby grins and folds her arms. 'Exactly, Max. Exactly,' she says. 'This is the problem with Captain Kickbutt …'

'Oh, don't start on about this again.'

But she has. She's started. And she keeps going.

YOU CAN'T JUST RUN AROUND THUMPING STUFF. WE DON'T EVEN KNOW WHO THE BAD GUY IS. THERE'S NO ONE TO THUMP.

I CAN THINK OF SOMEONE.

'We have to use our brains to solve a crime like this,' Abby continues. 'Like my mum does. Like Hailey Plum.'

'That's ridiculous,' I say. 'How is your brain going to chase a bad guy down the street? How is your mind going to snatch the necklace out of their hand? How are you going to defeat the evil merman Hammerhead in his flying stealth-submarine just by thinking about it? Answer me that, Abby Purcell!'

For someone who is very smart, Abby can say some very silly things.

Her mouth is wide open. 'I'm sorry … a flying … *what*?'

'I don't have time for this, do I, Tyson?' I sigh.

Tyson takes that as his cue. Time to switch to bodyguard mode. He pushes in between Abby and me, standing awkwardly close.

HE REALLY DOESN'T. HE'S A MOVIE STAR NOW.

'What are you doing?' Abby screws up her face.

'He can't answer any more of your questions.' Tyson folds his arms. 'Unless this is an approved interview for the press junket?'

'What's a junket?' I ask.

'I don't know.' Tyson frowns. 'I just hear my dad say it sometimes. It sounds like junk food though, so it must be good.'

That's good enough for me. I peek over Tyson's shoulder at Abby.

'I tell you what, if Hailey Plum is so good at solving crimes, then you should be able to solve the mystery of the stolen necklace, right?' I challenge her, pointing to the jewellery store. 'Just do it exactly like she would do it.'

Abby raises one eyebrow. 'Maybe I will,' she says.

'Maybe you won't.'

Abby squints. 'You know, speaking of wanting to thump people …'

6 Sometimes I think our teacher thinks we're stupid.

Miss Sweet looks like someone stole her lunch. Our teacher is not happy.

'Home,' she says slowly. She knows that's not a full sentence, right? I assume she does. Teachers know things like that. She just seems to be speaking very slowly. 'Work.'

I think that's it. I think that's all she's going to say.

Wait ... no, she's opening her mouth again. It seems like there's more.

'Eight letters,' she says. She's raising the volume a little bit now.

ONE WORD! SIMPLE CONCEPT. YOU TAKE THE WORK. YOU TAKE THE WORK HOME. YOU DO THE WORK. AT HOME. IT'S WORK. THAT YOU DO. AT HOME.

'I think you're really getting the hang of it, Miss Sweet,' I say without thinking.

Oops. She turns and looks straight at me. That was a bad idea.

'Max Walburt,' she says. 'If that's the case, then why is your book blank?'

UM ... ISN'T IT OBVIOUS?

I nod up towards the top of my head. Clearly I was busy yesterday with things that are much more important than homework.

'If you're talking about the fact that your head looks like a sea anemone ...' she says.

'Miss Sweet!' Pip exclaims, horrified.

It's okay, Pip. I can take it.

'I'll have you know,' I say, 'that this new haircut cost me three weeks of Hugo's pocket money! It is the definition of cool.'

Miss Sweet raises her eyebrows. 'Did you ask them to make it look like a toilet brush?'

'It's called style, people!' I exclaim, standing up. 'I have style!'

* * * *

After school, it's time for my entourage and me to head to the set. My agent (otherwise known as Hugo), my bodyguard (otherwise known as Tyson) and my duck (otherwise known as Duck) head towards the *Captain Kickbutt* studio. Hugo now carries a clipboard and Tyson is wearing a black cap with *SECURITY* written across the front.

We need to find my trailer. All super-famous people (and old people going on holidays) have a trailer. It's where they live while they're filming their movie. A home away from home, if you like. I should probably tell my parents I won't be home for dinner.

We walk around the corner of the studio building and BAM!

I've walked straight into none other than Spencer Daniels, Famous Kid, who appears to be walking and using his phone at the same time. His enormous bodyguard looms like a shadow behind him.

'Whoops. Eyes up, buddy!' I say. 'It's very dangerous to walk and use a phone at the same time. You might fall in a hole.'

Spencer Daniels rubs his head and looks at me as though I'm an awful-tasting sandwich.

'Excuse me?' he says, screwing up his face even more. 'Why do I have to talk to you?'

Well. That's a bit rude. I'm going to choose to ignore it. Clearly he's annoyed about being replaced as Captain Kickbutt. We've all had bad days.

'How come you're still here anyway?' I ask and then I realise. 'Oh, are you going to be an extra?'

Spencer Daniels chokes on the imaginary awful sandwich. He coughs and splutters.

ME? AN EXTRA? DO YOU KNOW WHO I AM?

YEAH, YOU'RE THAT KID WHO CAME SECOND ON -

'I'm the *star* of this movie!' he interrupts. 'Now move out of my way.'

Why do people like this kid? There's no way I'm moving out of his way. He can move out of my way.

'You can't really be the star any more though. Not when I'm Captain Kickbutt,' I say.

'You? How could you be Captain Kickbutt? You're not famous.'

Like a great agent, Hugo leaps in with some fact-checking.

HE ACTUALLY IS QUITE FAMOUS. HE'S THE FUNNY KID.

Spencer Daniels is new to Redhill. He clearly doesn't know that I am the most famous eleven-year-old here.

'The *funny* kid?' Spencer repeats, looking me up and down. Why does everyone in Hollywood do that? Slowly he starts to nod. 'That makes sense. He does look funny. What's the deal with your hair?'

'It's called *style*,' Hugo explains.

'No. It's not.'

All right, I'm beginning to get a bit fed up with this Famous Kid. You can be as talented as you like, but none of that matters if you're a twit. Besides, this kid hasn't even said one funny thing! Where's the sense of humour, Spencer Daniels?

'I think the director just wanted me to make the *Captain Kickbutt* movie a bit funnier,' I say. 'Plus, I can do the voice really well.'

'This movie is not a comedy,' Famous Kid replies. He looks offended by the idea. 'It's dark and dramatic.'

Oh, no. See, this is what's wrong with superhero movies. As soon as they take themselves too seriously, they stop being fun! Superhero movies *have* to be fun! If you're going to have people running around in colourful tights, you can't spend the whole movie being sad. Is that really what this kid is going to do to my favourite superhero?

'No!' I exclaim. 'Don't wreck Captain Kickbutt! He's the best superhero of all time. He has to be funny!'

Spencer Daniels' mouth is hanging open. He's like a statue. Maybe he's trying to catch flies. I don't understand what's happening.

Finally he speaks. 'I can't remember why I'm still talking to you,' he says. Then he turns to his bodyguard. 'Fridge?'

Suddenly the looming giant steps forward in front of Famous Kid. The Fridge bends over and stretches out one enormous arm like a boom gate. Then he starts to turn it, pivoting and collecting Hugo, Tyson and me, slowly sliding us out of the way.

I can hear him growling softly as though he's powered by a motor somewhere inside that humungous chest.

I look over at my bodyguard. Shouldn't *he* be doing something right about now?

He's got a huge grin on his face and he's staring adoringly at The Fridge.

'Hi,' Tyson says. Is he blushing? 'I'm Tyson. I'm his bodyguard.'

The Fridge ignores him. Once he has slid us across to the side, he nods at Spencer as if to say, 'Your path is clear, sir.' Famous Kid walks through, looking at his phone again. Has he learnt nothing?

On the other hand, I'd be completely fine with him falling in a hole right now.

'It's a real honour to finally meet you,' Tyson calls out after The Fridge. 'I'm a big fan.'

The Fridge ignores him. He doesn't seem like much of a talker. Mind you, if I had to follow someone as rude as Spencer Daniels around all day I'd probably lose the desire to speak too.

'Well, he's about as witty as wallpaper,' I say. 'Come on, let's go find my trailer.'

'Are you really sure the director said that you had the part?' Hugo asks. 'Because no one seems to have told Famous Kid yet.'

'Of course,' I say. 'I mean … I guess I was slightly unconscious at the time …'

Tyson is looking wistfully over his shoulder as we walk, whispering to himself:

HE'S JUST SO AWESOME …

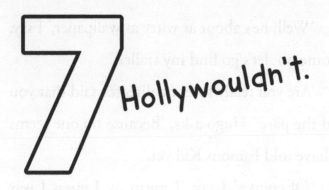

7 Hollywouldn't.

All right. This is getting ridiculous. Where is my trailer?

I spot Parakeet coming out of one of the studio doors with his clipboard in hand. I am about to call out to him when I remind myself that his name is not actually Parakeet. I mean, probably not. It would be funny if it did turn out to be Parakeet, but I think it's probably better if I don't take that chance.

'Good afternoon, Mr ...' I call out. Parakeet looks up from whatever he's been reading on his clipboard and sees my entourage. He looks a little surprised.

YOU GOT ASKED TO COME BACK?

YOU SHOULD REMEMBER. RAD DEFINITELY SAID COME BACK ON MONDAY AND SOMETHING ABOUT ME BEING THE NEW YOUNG CAPTAIN KICKBUTT. YOU SHOULD SEE MY NAME WRITTEN ON YOUR SHEET THERE.

Parakeet looks at his clipboard again. He scans the list. He flicks over and looks at a second sheet of paper.

HMMM, I CAN SEE A SQUIRT MCBUTTFACE ON HERE. IS THAT YOU?

I scowl. Apparently Parakeet is a little smarty-pants.

'My name is Max Walburt, thank you very much,' I say. 'I'm sure you'll see me on the *Ellen* show soon. Is it next week, Hugo?' I ask, throwing to my agent.

'Ah ...'

Come on, Hugo. You've got to be ready. Always ready.

'Never mind,' I say.

Parakeet checks the list again and then shakes his head. 'You're not on here.'

Tyson steps in front of me. I think he's been inspired by The Fridge.

IS THIS PUNK GIVING YOU TROUBLE, MAX?

Eek. I probably wouldn't call Parakeet a punk. We might still need him to sort this mess out.

Parakeet's eyes open very wide. 'Me?' he asks. 'I'm the assistant director of this movie. Are you sure you're talking about me?'

Tyson gulps.

'Look, we just need to know where my trailer is,' I say. 'Can you help us with that, Para … Mr Assistant Director?'

A crack of a smile appears on Parakeet's face as though I'd made a joke or something. I do make jokes all the time, but that wasn't supposed to be one.

'Your … *trailer*?' he asks as though he's trying to stop a laugh from popping out.

'What's so funny?' I ask. I assume my trailer's around here somewhere. All the big actors have them.

Parakeet bursts out laughing. He drops his clipboard.

'Your trailer!' he chuckles, wiping tears from his eyes with the back of his hand and bending down to pick up his clipboard. 'Of course. It was too big to go with the others, so they're going to reverse it in over here next to the bins. Just wait over there, next to that dumpster. It'll be here in just a few minutes.'

'Hey, Mr Assistant Director! We've been sitting here by this stinky dumpster the whole time!' I call out twenty minutes later when I spot Parakeet toddling by.

'I just checked in,' Parakeet calls back. 'You know how your trailer has a spa in the back? They had to refill it on the way here, so they got a little held up. Only a few more minutes, I'm sure.'

YOU'RE LYING ABOUT THE TRAILER, AREN'T YOU!

It's been another fifteen minutes. Something's starting to smell a bit fishy about all this, and it's not just the rubbish bin.

'I just got a message from them,' Parakeet yells back to us from the coffee cart. 'The donut pantry was a little low and they know how much you love donuts, so they're restocking it. Should be here any minute now!'

'I don't believe you!' I yell back.

'Mmmm, donuts,' my agent mumbles.

Rhonda Anderson Delaney is walking across the parking lot towards the main studio doors. Parakeet is scampering along beside her. I yell out to her. 'RAD! Parakeet, you're about to get fired. RAD!'

I run over towards the famous movie director. I'm a little puffed by the time I arrive.

'Oh, you're that kid who does his own stunts, right?' RAD says, gritting her teeth slightly. 'What was your name?'

MAX WALBURT. I'M NOT SURE WHAT'S GOING ON HERE, BUT HUGO IS MY AGENT AND HE'S NOT VERY HAPPY. MY TRAILER HAS NOT ARRIVED YET. WE'VE BEEN WAITING BY THESE BINS AND YOUR ASSISTANT DIRECTOR HAS BEEN VERY RUDE.

That's when I realise Rhonda Anderson Delaney is not really looking at my face. She's looking just above my face and pulling the expression you pull if you eat something sandy.

'What happened to your hair?' she asks.

Oh, this is getting ridiculous. Where is the focus around here? Aren't these people trying to create art with a multi-million-dollar budget?

'My hair is not the point!' I exclaim. 'I need to see the script and I'm sure I should have been called for wardrobe by now.'

The director looks from me to Parakeet, then back to me. 'Hmmm. Yes, it's difficult,' she says. 'There's a lot of waiting around in the film business, as I'm sure you know. Here's the thing, you're supposed to be in a scene with Hammerhead ...'

'My dad is playing Hammerhead,' Tyson interrupts. 'George Khan.'

'Yes, yes, I know,' RAD replies. 'There's this scene where Hammerhead has travelled back in time to catch Captain Kickbutt as a child, but he gets caught. The police are taking Hammerhead to the aquarium, because that's the best kind of jail for an evil merman, but there are long lines of people waiting for the aquarium toilets –'

'And I'll be helping the police?' I interject. 'Because I'm young Captain Kickbutt?'

Rhonda Anderson Delaney looks a little confused by that. 'Ah, no. You're going to be in the toilet queue in the background,' she says. 'You'll have to look like you desperately need to wee.'

'I'm sorry. What? You cast me as the new young Captain Kickbutt.'

'Ah, no. No, I didn't. You're an extra,' she says as though that's just a minor detail. 'The thing is, though, I don't know when we're going to shoot that scene because the fight scenes with young Captain Kickbutt and Hammerhead have been taking much longer than we thought. We probably won't get to it for a few days …'

'A few days?'

REPLACING MY HEAD?

I'm horrified.

'Yeah, it's amazing what they can do. When they're finished, no one will even know that it's you.' Then she grins. As though that's a good thing.

'But that's –'

'Anyway,' she says, like that's that, 'just hang around for a few days and we'll see if we get to it. Thinking about it, I might just cut the whole scene anyway. Don't worry. Someone will let you know.'

And just like that, she walks off. *Walks off!*

This is dreadful. I need to call my union. I turn back to Parakeet. He has a massive smile on his face.

'Sorry,' he says. He's not sorry. 'I'm going to cancel your trailer now.'

* * * *

My entourage and I walk slowly out of the studio. Even Duck looks dejected.

I'm in shock. I don't believe it. After all this work, I'm not even going to be an *extra* in the *Captain Kickbutt* movie. I'm not going to become a celebrity. I'm going to pretend to go to the toilet and then be turned into an unrecognisable girl! What's the point in being a celebrity if no one knows who you are?

Why does Rhonda Anderson Delaney get to decide these things anyway?

Across the parking lot, we see Spencer Daniels walking towards his trailer wearing a young Captain Kickbutt costume.

WOAH! LOOK, MAX, HE'S CAPTAIN KICKBUTT!

He does look very cool with his jetpack and the laser guns on his wrists. Why does that kid get to run around like a superhero and I don't? Especially when he's such a ... *not-nice person*!

What would Captain Kickbutt do if someone told him he couldn't be what he wanted to be? Would he let the evil trio of Rhonda Anderson Delaney, Parakeet and Famous Kid stop him? Would he take no for an answer this easily?

YEAH, PITY YOU'RE NOT REALLY GOING TO BE IN THE MOVIE.

I WOULDN'T BE SO SURE ABOUT THAT, TYSON. THIS IS NOT OVER.

SECURITY

8

Toilet ambushes are the best kind of ambushes.

'Hey, you guys!' Pip calls out. 'Dad's going to introduce me to Spencer Daniels. Want to come?'

We've arrived back at the studio the next afternoon because I've been working on something all day. Something Spencer Daniels probably won't want to see.

We see Pip and her dad, George Khan (also known as Hammerhead), walking across the carpark towards Spencer Daniels' trailer. Yes, that's right. He's got a trailer. All the kids were talking about it at school today. Apparently it's got gaming consoles, an air-hockey table and an ice-cream machine inside.

'Nah, it's all right,' I call back. 'We've already met him.'

Tyson looks at me. He really wants to go, I can tell by the look on his face. His eyes are pleading with me. He's desperate for the chance to see The Fridge in action again. Tyson hasn't stopped talking about his favourite human appliance all day long.

'Go on then,' I say to him. Hopefully I won't need a bodyguard to help me deliver my little creation to Rhonda Anderson Delaney. The only thing Hugo and I will need to do is get by Parakeet.

We find him near the bathrooms. Actually, he seems to be going *into* the bathroom, so we follow him and wait patiently right outside his cubicle. When he flushes the toilet and opens the door, we're right there.

'Hello, Mr Assistant Director,' I say. 'How are you today?'

Parakeet doesn't look too thrilled to see us.

WERE YOU WAITING FOR ME TO COME OUT OF THE TOILET?

'We just need to see the director,' Hugo explains. 'Can you tell us where she is?'

'I need to wash my hands,' he says, but we block his way to the sink.

'Just tell us where we can find RAD and we'll let you wash your hands,' I say, with a grin.

'That's disgusting.' Parakeet grimaces. 'You can't stop me washing my hands!'

'Where is she, Para ... Mr Assistant Director?'

'She's directing a movie. You can't see her. What are you holding?' He edges to the right, trying to get around us. We shuffle across so he can't.

'Something to help her see the light,' I explain.

'Why don't you show me and then I'll take it to her?' he says and scampers across to the left. We block him that way too.

'Promise?' Hugo asks. He nods.

'You wouldn't lie to a kid, would you?'

'Of course not,' Parakeet replies.

Hmmm … this is a tricky situation. How do I know he's not lying about not lying? I guess I don't have a lot of choice.

'We made her a poster,' I say and show it to him. 'Miss Sweet always gets us to make posters for class assignments so we thought we'd make a poster about why I should be young Captain Kickbutt and not Spencer What's-His-Face.'

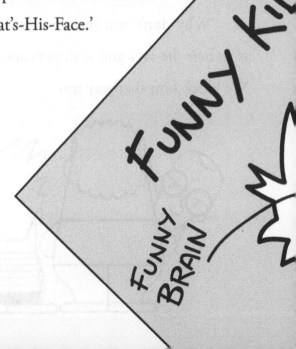

FAMOUS KID
FUNNY HAIR BUT!
NOT FUNNY BRAIN
ACTUALCY NO BRAIN!
STUPIDNESS EXPERT!
VERY VERY VERY HANDSOME
CAPTAIN KICKBUTT EXPERT!
by MAX (and Hugo)

'Wow! This is excellent!' Parakeet says.

'Really?' I ask. I must admit, I'm a little surprised. I thought he might not be so keen on it.

'It's genius,' he says. 'I'll give this to RAD and let you know. I really think this could change her mind.'

I look at Hugo and smile.

'Well you, sir, are free to wash your hands!' I move out of his way. He uses the sink and then turns back to us.

'So can I take this to her?'

'Of course,' I reply and hand him the poster.

He rips it in half. And then rips it in half again.

Our mouths drop open.

Then he throws the four bits in the bathroom bin. He sticks his tongue out at us, blows a raspberry and leaves.

Well, that last bit was a little immature.

9 What is a shakespeare?

Hugo, Duck and I leave the studio and begin to hatch a plan as we walk home. The best way to start a plan is to give Hugo an inspirational speech.

'It's time to go back to the drawing board,' I announce. 'It seems like they are not going to give me the role of young Captain Kickbutt after all. This is a mistake, of course, but one we cannot change at this time. However, they *will* let me on the set as an extra. This is an opportunity we cannot miss. Forget all this toilet queue stuff, I need a starring role! One in which they cannot change my head into a girl's head. We need to find a way for me to stand out on set and somehow become even more famous than Famous Kid. It's time for ideas. Go!'

I look at Hugo. He does seem inspired.

'No, he's a person. A guy. He wrote plays,' Hugo says. 'Actors always do Shakespeare when they want to impress people.'

'They do?'

'Sure. They hold a skull out in front of them and say, "To be or not to be, that is the question."'

I look at Hugo, feeling very confused.

'It's from Shakespeare,' he insists. 'You could hold a Hammerhead action figure in front of you and say, "To kick butt or not to kick butt, that is the question."'

'But that's never a question,' I say.

'Good point.' Hugo nods.

We're walking towards Goldstein's Jewellery. Even days after the robbery, it's still blocked off with police tape and there are TV cameras out the front. I can see Sergeant Purcell making some sort of statement. The one thing you can be sure of when Sergeant Purcell is around is that –

WHAT ARE YOU IDIOTS UP TO?

– Abby is here somewhere.

And here she is – the only person in the world who calls me idiot as if it's my actual name. For some reason, she's holding a magnifying glass.

'We're working out how we can impress the movie director and get Max a better role,' Hugo explains.

'More importantly, why are you here?' I ask and nod towards the magnifying glass.

'I'm looking for clues,' Abby says as though it's obvious. I have no idea what she's talking about. We stand there in awkward silence for a moment. She realises I'm not getting it. 'The robbery. Remember that?'

'Oh, yeah, you're going to try to solve it,'

I say. Good for her.

THERE ARE STILL LOTS OF NEWSPAPERS AND TV CAMERAS AROUND. THAT'S GOOD FOR YOUR PARENTS' SHOP, ISN'T IT, HUGO?

THEY GOT ROBBED, ABBY. NONE OF THIS IS GOOD FOR THEIR SHOP.

OH, SURE. I WAS JUST THINKING, IT COULD TURN OUT FOR THE BEST. DON'T YOU THINK?

Hugo and I look at each other, confused.

'Abby, have you been eating a glue stick? What are you talking about?' I ask. 'And what's with the magnifying glass? You know you can just get a phone and zoom in on the camera. There are apps for that.'

She glares at us. 'Hailey Plum carries a magnifying glass wherever she goes. She always returns to the scene of the crime after everything has died down to see what may have been missed. For example, did you know that the cable for the security cameras in the jewellery store had been cut the afternoon before the robbery?'

'Yes,' Hugo replies. 'I did know that.'

Abby squints. 'Oh, did you, Hugo?'

She writes something down in her little notebook. It seems that Abby has gone crazy on Hailey Plum fumes and now she's suspicious of everybody.

'And nothing says "exciting" like a jigsaw,' I say sarcastically. Anyway, we're getting distracted. We did not come here to talk to Abby about the case. We have much more important work to do. 'Come on, Hugo, we need to work out something that I can do for the movie that will make them give me a starring role.'

Hugo scratches his head. 'I think you should show them that you can cry immediately if the director asks you to. All actors can do that and it's very difficult,' he says.

'Can you do that, Max?' Abby asks. 'Can you cry on cue?'

'Sure,' I lie.

'Show me.' Abby smirks.

Uh-oh.

'I'm not going to do it now,' I say.

Abby raises one eyebrow. 'You can't do it.'

'Can so.'

'I don't believe you,' she says, crossing her arms.

'Fine,' I say. Then I lift my right leg and stomp on my left toe. 'Ow!'

Argh! I've got tears in my eyes all right. That hurt way more than I thought it would.

'That doesn't count!' Abby protests.

It most certainly should count. I almost broke my own toe for no reason. What, I don't get any credit for that? I clear my throat.

'It's how they do it in the movies,' I say.

Abby is not impressed. Maybe she needs to look at my toe with her magnifying glass.

'Max! Hugo! Wait up!'

We turn around and see Tyson running to catch up with us. He must have finally finished hanging out with The Fridge.

'I know what you can do to get into the movie!'

10

Parakeet
vs
Duck.

We follow Tyson all the way back to the *Captain Kickbutt* studio. By the time we get there it's almost dark. We walk across the parking lot until we can see a side door in the old chicken soup warehouse. I can see Parakeet pacing back and forth in front of it while he talks to someone on his mobile phone.

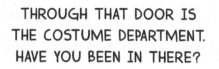

THROUGH THAT DOOR IS THE COSTUME DEPARTMENT. HAVE YOU BEEN IN THERE?

NO.

DAD SHOWED IT TO ME THIS AFTERNOON. THERE ARE ALL THESE AMAZING COSTUMES INSIDE. MASKS, CAPES, SUITS. IT'S A SUPERHERO MOVIE, RIGHT? SO IT'S FULL OF SUPERHERO COSTUMES IN ALL SORTS OF DIFFERENT SIZES.

'Cool,' I say. That does sound pretty amazing. I'm used to making Captain Kickbutt costumes out of ice-cream containers and a dressing gown.

'All we have to do is sneak in there and ... *borrow* a cool superhero costume for you,' Tyson suggests.

THAT'S EPIC, BUT REMIND ME, HOW IS THAT GOING TO GET ME IN THE MOVIE?

'Have you heard of improv?' Tyson asks. I shake my head. 'My dad talks about it all the time. It's a game actors play. They love it. It's acting but without a script. One person just starts and everyone else has to go along with it.'

'That sounds like how we play Captain Kickbutt,' Hugo says.

TOMORROW, WHEN THEY'RE FILMING A SCENE WITH YOUNG CAPTAIN KICKBUTT AND HAMMERHEAD, YOU JUMP INTO THE SCENE AS A BRAND-NEW SUPERHERO AND START IMPROVISING. JUST MAKE UP WHATEVER YOU WANT. THEY'LL PLAY ALONG AND THE DIRECTOR WILL ALREADY BE FILMING THE WHOLE THING. IF YOU MAKE IT FUNNY, SHE'LL END UP FILMING THIS HILARIOUS SCENE WITH YOU AS THIS BRAND-NEW KID SUPERHERO, AND SHE'LL DECIDE SHE WANTS TO KEEP YOUR NEW CHARACTER IN THE MOVIE AND THAT IT SHOULD BE A COMEDY AFTER ALL. THE NEXT THING YOU KNOW, YOU'LL BE AS FAMOUS AS PEPPA PIG!

'Tyson, you're a genius,' I whisper. I love it. A brand-new superhero means I'll have dialogue, fight scenes and special effects. I'll probably even be on the poster. 'Now, all we need to do is get past Parakeet over there.'

'We need a diversion,' Tyson says. We all look at each other and then slowly we all turn to Duck. Has there ever been a greater distraction in the history of the world than Duck?

I crouch down to explain to Duck what we need him to do, but he just waddles off in the direction of Parakeet. Sometimes I forget that he's listening to everything the whole time.

Parakeet is arguing with someone on the phone about the soundtrack. 'The music you sent is too light and … fluffy. I know that's not a musical word, but it sounds like, you know, *twiddly-twiddly-tweet-tweet*. But this is a serious superhero movie. It's dark and full of complex themes and frustration. We need the music to be more *dom-dom-dom-dahhhh*! Does that make sense?'

Suddenly Parakeet gets pecked on the ankle by a duck.

'Argh!' he screams and obviously confuses the person on the other end of the phone. 'No, no, not horror music. Aarrgghh! Sorry, there's a duck. No, not a cartoon duck. A real duck. There's a duck biting my – Aaarrrggghhh!'

Duck starts to chase Parakeet around in circles.

'Let's go,' I whisper to Hugo and Tyson, and we run across the carpark towards the door.

'Stop biting me! Why is there a duck here anyway? Argh! What are you doing? You can't have a piggyback!'

We look over as we get to the door and, sure enough, Duck has jumped up on Parakeet's back and is holding on for dear life. Is he trying to grab the phone? I think he's trying to grab the phone!

NO, I'M NOT TRYING TO TELL YOU I WANT QUACKS IN THE SOUNDTRACK! WHY WOULD I WANT QUACKS IN THE MUSIC FOR *CAPTAIN KICKBUTT*? THERE ISN'T EVEN A DUCK IN THE *CAPTAIN KICKBUTT* MOVIE! WHAT DO YOU MEAN, 'THEN WHY DO I KEEP YELLING ABOUT A DUCK?' BECAUSE THERE'S ONE ON TOP OF ME!

I grab the door handle and pull open the door. We need to get inside before we all burst out laughing!

We disappear inside just as we hear Parakeet yell one final time. 'I'll call you quack! I mean, I'll call you back!'

We did it! I don't believe it.

'That duck is one awesome little bird,' Tyson says with a grin.

'You don't know the half of it,' I agree.

'All right, follow me,' Tyson says.

We're in a corridor that's lit only by EXIT signs. Tyson takes us to a room and it's like we've entered Fancy Dress Heaven.

The Costume Department! There are rows and rows of clothes on hangers, but not just clothes. Superhero costumes! Capes! Masks! Body armour! Helmets! Swords! Guns! Shields! Boots! Gloves! Spandex suits! They even have them in all sorts of different sizes.

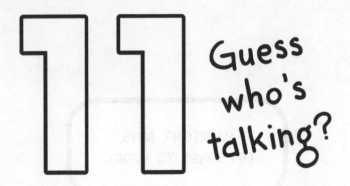

11 Guess who's talking?

The next morning, Mrs Sniggles, our principal, calls a surprise school assembly.

At Redhill Middle School, assemblies mean that the whole school is taken into the hall where we are forced to sit on the floor and listen to teachers talk at us through squealing microphones. Often we get into trouble for something, then Abby usually wins an award of some kind and then we sleep through the rest of it while our bums go numb. I don't know why we do this. I assume the teachers must enjoy it or something.

Now, as the funny kid at Redhill Middle

School, I have a reputation to protect. You only get to be the funny kid if you do funny things.

Today, I've come to school expecting to spend it perfecting my plan to crash the *Captain Kickbutt* set this afternoon, but when an opportunity to play pranks at the school assembly comes along, you have to jump at the chance.

There's an idea I've been wanting to try for a while.

MISS SWEET? I'M BUSTING!

She glares at me as only teachers can. She starts to say, 'No,' and then changes that to, 'Why didn't you go before?' and then she rolls her eyes as though she can't remember why she climbed out of bed this morning and says, *Just go then!'*

I stand up and tiptoe quickly to the end of the row, darting out through the side door of the hall.

Only I'm not going to the bathroom. I didn't lie. I never said I needed to pee. I said I was busting. Busting to play a prank on Mr Bert, who's currently making an incredibly long and boring announcement about lost property!

If people wanted their property back, Mr Bert, they wouldn't have lost it in the first place!

I run around the back of the hall and sneak in through the fire exit behind the stage. It's dark back here and I can hear Mr Bert droning on about how many lunch boxes there are in the lost property bin. The kids of Redhill need rescuing and who better to do it than the funny kid?

I find the sound system. This is the place where Mr Bert's microphone lead is plugged in. Next to the plug is a volume knob. Beside it is another identical plug with another volume knob. I reach into the box of equipment that's next to the sound system and pull out a spare microphone and a spare lead. I put this into the second plug and slowly turn up the volume knob until it matches Mr Bert's microphone. Now, the microphone I am holding is turned up just as loud as the one that Mr Bert is using.

I peek through the curtain and see him holding up a pink lunch box to show everyone the sorts of things that are in the lost property bin.

I get ready to do my best Mr Bert voice. Then I turn the volume down on his microphone and start talking into mine – pretending to be Mr Bert.

'Ah, this here is my pink lunch box,' I say. I hear people giggle. They can no longer hear Mr Bert talking because his microphone doesn't work. They can only hear my voice.

MY MUMMY GAVE IT TO ME WHEN I WAS SIX AND I'VE EATEN MY LUNCH OUT OF IT EVERY DAY SINCE. I LIKE THE LITTLE CHEESE STICKS. DO YOU LIKE CHEESE STICKS? MY MUMMY LIKES CHEESE STICKS AND I LIKE MY MUMMY.

The whole assembly is laughing now.

Mr Bert is trying to work out what is going on. Where is the voice coming from and why can no one hear him? He's looking around everywhere.

'What? What's going on?' I say, still pretending to be Mr Bert.

WHY ARE YOU ALL LAUGHING? DID YOU HEAR ME FART? IT WAS SUPPOSED TO BE A SILENT FART, BUT WHEN IT CAME OUT, IT MADE A LITTLE TOOT!

The whole assembly is in hysterics! This is too good.

And then onto the stage marches Mrs Sniggles.

Uh-oh.

I put my microphone down and turn the volume on Mr Bert's microphone back up. When the principal arrives at the lectern, the microphone is working just fine.

'That's enough! Quieten down,' comes her grandma voice. Mrs Sniggles may be this tiny grandma of an old lady, but she has a mysterious way of making sure everyone listens to her all the time. It's some crazy magic, that's for sure.

What I'm *not* going to do is play my prank on her! It might be time for me to head back to my seat.

'I don't know what happened here, but that's quite enough,' Mrs Sniggles says as Mr Bert shuffles off the stage, looking very confused. 'We have a very special treat for you today, Redhill Middle School, not that you deserve it. We have a special guest visiting our assembly to inspire you to chase your dreams.'

I stop before I get to the fire exit. Who could the special guest be?

I'D LIKE YOU TO GIVE A BIG REDHILL MIDDLE SCHOOL WELCOME TO THE VERY TALENTED, VERY FAMOUS SPENCER DANIELS!

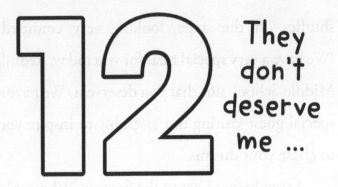

12

They don't deserve me ...

I scamper back to the curtain and watch as Spencer Daniels steps onto the stage and walks across to the microphone stand. There are loud gasps from the audience and then cheering! I can see the students' faces from here. They're smiling and pointing and talking to each other about how cool it is to have a really famous actor at *their* school assembly.

Famous Kid taps the microphone to check that it's working. 'Is this on?' he asks.

'Yes!' the whole school replies in one giant, cheesy chorus.

'Mum! Make sure you're filming this. Are

you filming it?' Spencer asks. He looks in the direction of his mum, who is holding up her phone to capture her son's speech on video. She's nodding like her head's on a spring. He explains, 'This is going to be pretty inspiring stuff, so we'll probably put it on YouTube. You guys don't mind going viral, do you?'

'No!' they reply in an even more pathetic display of starstruck-dom.

'You're awesome, Spencer Daniels!' someone yells out. I think it was Pip.

'Well, I have a simple message for you today, ordinary kids. You can become extra-ordinary like me. All you need to do is believe in your heart that you can do it.'

Oh, spew! What is this rubbish? He can't really think that this is going to inspire people, can he?

YOU SEE, I USED TO BE ORDINARY. LIKE YOU. BUT I ALWAYS KNEW IN MY HEART THAT I WAS MEANT TO BE SOMETHING GREATER. I ALWAYS KNEW THAT I WAS BETTER THAN OTHER PEOPLE.

I look out at the audience and they're sitting there with huge smiles on their faces. That doesn't make any sense. Why would they listen to this kid? He's horrible!

A few minutes ago, all the kids at Redhill were laughing at my prank and now they've forgotten what real talent looks like. They're staring hopelessly at this nincompoop just because someone said he's famous.

I think it might be time to intervene.

I walk back over to the sound system and pick up the second microphone.

'When you've got a gift like I do, you need to share it with the world. But only if it's awesome. And if I can be honest with you here today, you might think you've got a gift, but you're probably wrong. The chances are pretty high that you are not awesome. You just think you are. I can understand that, looking at someone like me, it must seem like it's easy to be this cool …'

They're nodding. Like they're agreeing with him! Oh, I can't take this any more.

I turn his volume down and use my best Spencer Daniels voice to take over this ridiculous speech. 'Well, it *is* easy to be this cool,' I say. I watch Famous Kid freeze. I keep going.

IN FACT, IT'S SO EASY, I DON'T DO ANYTHING EXCEPT … PICK MY NOSE. AND EAT IT.

This should liven things up a bit. I look through the curtain. People seem annoyed.

Oh, come on, lighten up, everybody! Where's your sense of humour gone? Don't tell me Spencer Daniels took it! I continue.

'I like to sing love songs to my cat. That's how I got on the TV talent show. All you girls thought I was singing love songs to you, but that's not true. I'm in love with my cat.'

'Boo!'

What? I look back out through the curtain. Spencer Daniels has stepped away from the microphone and is folding his arms and tapping his foot. The audience of kids are booing me! They'd actually prefer to hear from Famous Kid than Funny Kid!

Okay, I've had about enough of this. This is my turf! My school! Famous Kid doesn't get to just turn up and become more popular than the Funny Kid just … *because*!

'Turn his microphone back on!' kids are yelling.

All right. Fine. You want Famous Kid instead of Funny Kid, Redhill Middle School? You can have him.

I turn his microphone back on and drop mine. I turn around and head towards the fire exit.

Only the exit is blocked.

By The Fridge.

13 Short stuff.

Now would probably be a good time to … RUN!

The problem is, where do I run to? There's only one exit back here and The Fridge is blocking it. If I run out onto the stage, everyone will see me! Most of the time that's fine – I love being the centre of attention – but in this case I'd rather Mrs Sniggles not have proof that the microphone prank was down to me.

The Fridge takes a step towards me, one giant hand outstretched as though he wants to pop my head off my body with his thumb like it's a drink-bottle lid.

This is probably as good a time as any to take

a little pause and talk about what it's like being a short kid.

I've been short since I was born. I've always thought it interesting that you can't be born tall, you can only be born long. And once you're a standing-up human, you can't be long, you can only be tall. But in both situations, if you are the opposite, you are short. Well, I have always been short.

This is annoying most of the time. You can't go on the big rides at the theme park. When you wear shorts, they look like long pants and when you wear long pants, the extra material makes you look like a seal. Also, everyone's always telling you you have dandruff.

Sometimes I'm not even tall enough to see onto the page.

There is perhaps only one advantage to being short. It's hard for tall people to catch you.

And The Fridge, as you can see, is as tall as … a fridge.

I do a slide to my left. He turns like a robot.

I do a slide to my right. He turns like a robot.

I do a forward roll into a stack of chairs.

Oops. Didn't mean to do that.

I hear Spencer Daniels stop his speech. He had just been in the middle of saying something about how you should chase your dreams, but only if you're as good as him.

I'm too busy being chased by his bodyguard to chase my dreams.

The Fridge starts pulling chairs off the top of the pile.

I start to crawl for the door on my hands and knees. He tries to reach down to grab me, but if he leans too far forward, his upper body will be too heavy for his lower body and he'll topple over.

I scramble for the door, pull it open and run out into the sunshine … OOF!

I've run straight into Tyson.

'Miss Sweet sent me to come find you,' he says. 'She thinks you've fallen in the toilet. I knew you must have been messing around back there.'

'Quick!' I say, pointing to the door. 'Stop him!'

'Stop who?'

Suddenly the door flies open and there is The Fridge.

'Him!' I yell and hide behind Tyson.

'Woah, he's so cool,' Tyson says.

'No, he's not! He's trying to squash me!' I whisper.

'Mr Fridge!' Tyson calls out.

Doesn't he know he has a job to do? Doesn't he know he's supposed to be on *my* side?

'You are a terrible bodyguard!' I yell, just as Miss Sweet steps out from the hall and glares across at us.

'You two! Back in here now!'

The way she's glaring, not even The Fridge is going to mess with her.

14 Do not tumble dry!

I'm hiding inside a washing machine.

Not a real washing machine. You should never do that! Are you crazy?

It's a fake movie washing machine and no one knows I'm in here. Outside the washing machine, young Captain Kickbutt (Spencer Daniels) and Hammerhead (Pip and Tyson's dad) are in the middle of filming a scene in a laundromat. The filming lights are bright. The cameras are rolling. There's a fuzzy microphone on a stick hanging over everyone's heads.

And I am waiting for my moment.

My moment of stardom.

That no one knows is coming.

I'm dressed in my stolen superhero costume and I'm ready to give this improv thing a crack. Somewhere out there beyond the cameras, Tyson is watching on.

'You'll never find the pearls, Captain Kickbutt!' Hammerhead says from where he's standing beside the washing machine. 'I have hidden them in an invisibility capsule in the Pacific Ocean sometime in the future.'

'The Bermuda Pearls belong in the National History Museum, Hammerhead!' Young Captain

Kickbutt replies. Spencer is putting on this gravelly voice, but between you and me, he hasn't got it. I hope they can fix it later. Maybe I'll come in to the studio and they can record me saying his lines instead. 'They're not yours to take!'

'They are now, little Captain Kickbutt, and there's nothing you can do about it!' Hammerhead says and throws some dirty

washing at the young superhero. Ew! I just saw someone's undies.

'Sure there is, Hammerhead,' says young Captain Kickbutt. 'I can kick your butt.'

That's my cue!

I push open the front of the washing machine and leap out! Well, actually, it doesn't quite go as smoothly as that. It's a pretty small door I have to climb through and I stumble and trip over my cape a little.

Either way, I end up standing, feet apart, fists on my hips in full superhero pose.

'Not so fast, Captain Kickbutt!' I say in a loud voice. I'm not sure how good that fuzzy microphone is. I'd better speak up.

YOUR AUNT JANINE HAS BEEN ABDUCTED BY ALIENS. YOU NEED TO HELP ME RESCUE HER.

Young Captain Kickbutt doesn't reply. I look over at him. He has screwed up his face as though he's just smelt someone's fart.

'What?' Spencer Daniels says. He's not using his deep voice. 'Who are you? This is not in the script.'

'Just roll with it, buddy,' I whisper behind a gloved hand. Then, in my loud superhero voice: 'You remember Aunt Janine, don't you? She's the one who smells like peppermint tea!'

'Wha—'

'CUT!' It's the voice of Rhonda Anderson Delaney from somewhere in the darkness behind the lights. 'Cut! Cut!'

I remember the advice Tyson gave me just before I came in. He told me that the rules of the improvisation game are that you need to stay in the scene. Whatever happens, stay in the scene.

So … exactly what Spencer Daniels is *not* doing. This kid is a terrible actor!

'No, don't cut!' I yell back, keeping my superhero voice on. 'Aunt Janine is going to be vaporised on the planet Zorg if we don't rescue her. Forget Fishboy over here –' I point at Hammerhead the evil merman.

'Hey!' Hammerhead says. Evil mermen don't like being referred to as Fishboy.

I SAID CUT!

Rhonda Anderson Delaney steps in front of the lights into the scene. What's she doing? She's going to block the cameras. This is the most unprofessional film set I've ever worked on!

'You must protect the family, Captain Kickbutt!' I say,

running over and grabbing Captain Kickbutt by the shoulders and shaking him.

'Who is this kid?' The director is looking around as though someone should have an answer for that question. She doesn't get one. 'Get him off my set!'

This isn't really going the way that Tyson said it would. Oh, well, not much point stopping now.

KEEP IT ROLLING! WE'RE GETTING GOOD STUFF HERE. IT'S COMEDY GOLD! YOUNG CAPTAIN KICKBUTT, WORK WITH ME! I'M KINDA CARRYING THE WHOLE THING ON MY OWN HERE. WE NEED TO GET YOUR BUTTMOBILE AND GO FIND AUNT JANINE! YOU GET THE ANTI-ALIEN WEAPONS! I'LL GET THE SNACKS!

Spencer Daniels looks like someone just picked him up and transported him into a fantasy world constructed entirely of baked beans. He doesn't know what's going on. I don't think he's taken any acting classes in his life. He seems to have the imagination of a muddy puddle.

'Ah,' he stammers. 'I don't know what you're –'

OH, FOR FLUFFING FARTS! I THOUGHT YOU WERE SUPPOSED TO BE AN ACTOR!

Suddenly the director reaches out and tries to grab me by the arm. She misses because I'm a superhero.

'SECURITY!' Rhonda Anderson Delaney yells at the top of her lungs.

As I run around behind young Captain Kickbutt, he turns and follows me. I glance at his face and realise I've offended him with the 'I thought you were supposed to be an actor' comment. He's not an actor, after all. He's a talent show contestant who lots of people think is cute. He's probably feeling very inadequate. He looks like he might cry.

'But I am an act–' Spencer Daniels protests, but I interrupt him because there are more important things going on right now than his sense of self. For starters, the director is still trying to tackle me.

'Then you're supposed to be improv-ing with me, super-chump!' I say.

Young Captain Kickbutt looks like he's trying to remember the 'How to Be an Actor' videos he watched on YouTube.

'Ah –'

Suddenly, from somewhere behind the lights, something the size of a brontosaurus' backside appears out of nowhere. It's The Fridge again!

'Look out!' I yell. 'The Fridge at two o'clock!'

Spencer Daniels' bodyguard comes barrelling onto the set and charges straight for me. I backpedal across the fake laundromat until I trip over a merman's tail.

'Are you that kid who hangs out with my –' Hammerhead looks down and asks.

'Zip it, Fish Face!' I yell at him as I clamber back to my feet. This mask is doing a very good job at hiding my identity. The last thing I need right now is my friends' dad exposing my alter ego.

Anyway, stay in the scene, people! What is wrong with these actors? A new character has just entered the game – Mr Bodyguard over here. You can't just ignore a hulking mass like that.

Maybe they'll form a super team with me? That always happens in superhero movies.

'Why is no one fighting The Fridge?' I yell. 'He's the one who kidnapped Aunt Janine! Get him!'

Young Captain Kickbutt suddenly looks confused.

I THOUGHT AUNT JANINE WAS IN SPACE?

FINALLY YOU'RE CONTRIBUTING!

'Yes, she's on Planet Zorg. But The Fridge is an intergalactic Uber driver, aren't ya, big fella?'

I make a running slide for the tumble dryer, but I've misjudged it. A giant foot stomps down on my cape and halts my slide like a coat hanger around the throat.

'Ugh.'

Big hands grab me under the armpits. This must be how Batman felt when he fought Bane.

GOT YA, KID. YOU'RE DONE.

He slings me over his shoulder like a sack of potatoes and marches me off the set.

'Don't you ever set foot on my film set again!' Rhonda Anderson Delaney screams after us. I feel like this plan may have backfired.

'You don't know what you're missing out on!' I say. 'I just handed you a comic subplot on a silver platter!'

Apparently I'm the lone voice of reason around here.

As soon as we step outside the studio, The Fridge stops. I can't see much from where I am, slung over the back of his shoulder. All I hear are the words of my very own bodyguard.

'Put him down.'

The Fridge growls.

'You might be my idol,' Tyson says. 'But that kid is my friend. I said, put him down.'

Woah. Tyson's voice is so forceful that The Fridge just obeys. I would probably do whatever Tyson told me to if he spoke to me like that too.

The Fridge grunts and walks back towards the studio door.

'Thanks, Tyson. You have fully redeemed yourself. That was amazing. I thought I was going to end up as frozen leftovers for sure.'

Tyson just looks sad. He nods towards The Fridge, who disappears inside.

15 Spy catcher!

Tyson and I trudge to Palm Grove, Hugo's apartment block.

Today has turned out to be rather rubbish for both of us. Tyson betrayed his idol and I got fired from the *Captain Kickbutt* movie.

My hopes of being a movie star have been completely dashed. There are all these famous people in town and I am not one of them. Rhonda Anderson Delaney never wants to see me again and the whole of Redhill Middle School likes Famous Kid more than Funny Kid.

I kick a pebble into a bush.

'Ow!'

Tyson and I look at each other, wide-eyed. That bush just spoke.

TYSON, WE'VE DISCOVERED A MAGICAL BUSH.

Out climbs a very grumpy Abby Purcell.

'What did you do that for?' she asks as though *I'm* the weird one.

'What are you doing in a bush?' Tyson asks.

Suddenly Abby says, 'Shhh! Get back here!' She grabs our hands and pulls us behind the bush. I look over and see Hugo's dad getting out of his car across the road. 'I don't want them to see me!'

I'm confused.

'You know that's Hugo's apartment block, right?' I ask.

'Of course I do!' Abby says. She pulls out a set of binoculars.

'You're spying on Hugo?'

Abby doesn't answer. She just watches.

'Hailey Plum says it's always the person you least expect,' Abby whispers.

'You think Hugo robbed his parents' jewellery store?' Tyson asks.

YOU'VE OFFICIALLY LOST YOUR MIND, ABBY PURCELL! IN FACT, I THINK I SAW IT IN MR BERT'S LOST PROPERTY.

She takes a moment's break from the binoculars to glare at me. 'You have to use your head, Max. You should try it.' She pulls out a piece of paper covered in numbers. 'While you've been running around trying to be a movie star, I've been doing some real detective work.'

'You've been doing maths? For fun?' I ask.

'No! Although, sometimes,' she says. 'These are sales numbers from the jewellery store for the last six months. They say how well the shop has been doing. You know, whether it's been making any money for Hugo's parents.'

'How did you get this?' Tyson asks, taking a look.

'Never mind,' Abby replies. 'The point is, the shop hasn't been doing very well. But now? Now that the necklace has been stolen and the shop has been in the newspapers and on TV, it's become much more famous around Redhill. I went back and looked. They were on TV on Sunday and on the front page on Monday and Tuesday because of the robbery. That's pretty convenient, isn't it? I bet their shop is going to be selling a lot more now. So maybe Hugo was trying to help his parents? Maybe he's just hiding the necklace for a while and he'll give it back to them once everyone's forgotten about the robbery?'

Tyson and I stare at her with our mouths open.

'Abby Purcell, you have lost your mind,' I say. 'Not even Hailey Plum would be this dumb. Hugo would never rob his own parents' jewellery store. That's crazy! You keep saying Hailey Plum is so much smarter than Captain Kickbutt, but Captain Kickbutt would never be this stupid. He'd solve this crime by –'

Hang on a minute …

'By what …?' Abby asks. 'Max …? By what?'

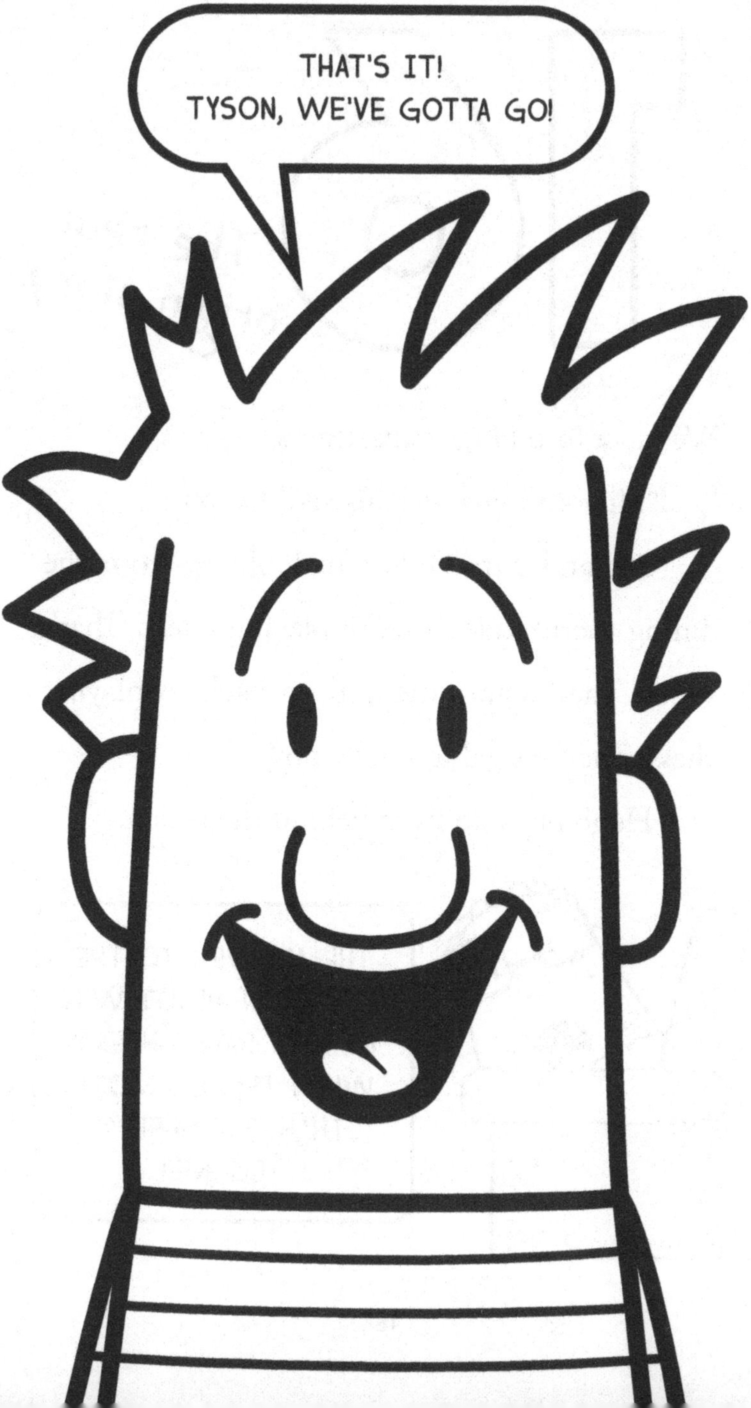
THAT'S IT!
TYSON, WE'VE GOTTA GO!

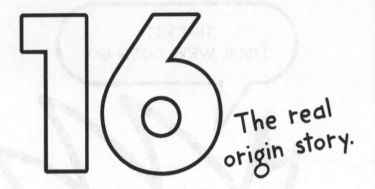

16

The real origin story.

We burst into Hugo's apartment.

'Hugo! I know the answer!' I shout.

Mr and Mrs Goldstein look up from the dining-room table. They're playing chess. That's sweet. They ignore me and go back to playing chess. They're used to me by now.

Hugo pops up from behind the couch.

THE ANSWER TO THE QUESTION ABOUT WHY NO ONE SAYS 'SHEEPS' WHEN THERE'S MORE THAN ONE SHEEP? TELL ME!

'No. It's got nothing to do with sheep,' I say and grab his arm, dragging him and Tyson down the hall. I can't have his parents hearing my plan. 'I know the answer to the question "How can I be super famous if I got fired from the *Captain Kickbutt* movie?"'

'Oh, right. Yes, good question,' Hugo says.

'I am also interested in the sheep one though, if you get to it,' Tyson adds.

I sit Hugo and Tyson down on Hugo's bed. It's safest there. I don't want them falling over in shock when I tell them my amazing idea.

I AM GOING TO BECOME A REAL SUPERHERO.

Hugo blinks.

'You're gonna what?' Tyson asks.

'I am going to become a real superhero,' I repeat. 'Forget Spencer Daniels and all his pretending. I'm going to be Redhill's first *real* superhero and I'm going to find out who stole the necklace from your parents' store, Hugo. I've already got the costume! You guys have to help me. Hugo, you can be my Norman.'

'Oh, not Norman again,' Hugo says, pulling a face. 'Max, I really don't like –'

'You're a naturally gifted Norman, Hugo. Don't fight Mother Nature. You'll lose,' I say. I'm feeling very excited about this idea. 'Now, you both have to help me because I need a name. A superhero name.'

I pull the superhero suit we borrowed from the costume department out of my backpack and lay it on the bed.

'Ooh, this'll be fun,' Hugo says. 'What about an animal? Lots of superheroes are named after animals. You could be SheepMan!'

'It needs to be a dangerous animal, Hugo. I can't be a sheep.'

'Do you know what one of the most dangerous animals in the world is that no one has named a superhero after?' Tyson says.

'What?'

'The Hippo.'

'I am not calling myself The Hippo!' I say.

'They are actually very dangerous,' Hugo says, agreeing with Tyson.

Outside, a storm is brewing. I hear thunder in the distance. That gives me an idea.

'What about … ThunderBolt?' I say.

'Ooh, that's good,' Hugo says.

'Yeah, I like that,' Tyson adds.

'Hey, Tyson, it's good there's a storm coming,' I say. 'It'll get rid of Abby from out the front.'

'Abby's out the front of my apartment block?' Hugo asks, surprised.

'Oh, yeah, it's so funny. She's spying on you. She thinks you robbed your parents' jewellery store,' I say and try to imagine the word ThunderBolt written across the front of the superhero suit.

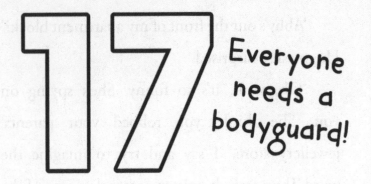

17 Everyone needs a bodyguard!

'Hey, can you paint ThunderBolt on the front and the cape?' I ask Hugo.

Hugo is pacing back and forth in his room. He doesn't seem to be paying much attention. 'I can't believe Abby thinks I did something so terrible. Why would she think that? She's going to get me in trouble.'

'Norman, I need you to focus on the costume!' I say.

'Don't worry about it, Hugo,' Tyson says. 'She's nuts. No one will believe her.'

Hugo looks at Tyson as though he's had an idea. 'I need you to be *my* bodyguard too!'

Tyson starts shaking his head before Hugo's even finished the sentence. 'I'm done being a bodyguard. I'm no good at it.'

'You're great at it!' I say, not looking up from my costume.

YOU DIDN'T SEE THE WAY THE FRIDGE LOOKED AT ME. HE WAS MY ROLE MODEL. HE WAS SO DISAPPOINTED IN ME.

Hugo takes a deep breath. 'You know, I once heard someone very wise say that when you've got a gift and you know you're better than other people, you need to share it with the world …'

I look up. I've heard this before recently.

Suddenly I remember and turn to Hugo. 'Are you trying to inspire Tyson by quoting Spencer Daniels and his terrible speech?'

Hugo shrugs. 'I actually thought it was quite good.'

'It wasn't "quite good",' I object. 'It was ridiculous! I can't believe –'

That's when we hear a door slam. It's the front door. Tyson has just left.

We race after him. He's marching across the street looking very inspired.

'Why is he yelling at that bush?' Hugo asks as we run down the front steps. By the time we get to the bottom, it becomes more obvious. Abby climbs out as we get closer.

'I'm Hugo's bodyguard and you need to get out of here. This is private property!' Tyson says. He's using that voice again. The one that worked so well on The Fridge.

'The street is not private property, Tyson,' Abby replies.

Abby's eyes open wide. She takes an actual step backward as though she's been given an electric shock. I'm not sure anyone has ever threatened to call Abby's mummy on her before.

'Well, um …'

Oh, wow. Abby Purcell is lost for words!

She shakes her head a little as though she's trying to get her focus back. It seems to work. She huffs and starts to walk away, but not before turning and pointing at all of us.

I WILL SOLVE THIS MYSTERY AND CATCH WHOEVER IT WAS WHO STOLE THAT NECKLACE. JUST WATCH ME!

18 The FAKE origin story.

'I finished your costume!' Hugo says when he and Tyson arrive in my dad's shed on Saturday morning. This is where we will be building my secret base.

He pulls the costume out of his backpack and holds it up.

Tyson and I gasp.

Oh, no.

'HUGO!'

'What?' Hugo asks, poking his head around from behind the costume. 'You don't like it?'

I point at the words he's written across the front of the superhero suit.

Do I really have to say it? Isn't the issue obvious? Tyson helps me out.

Hugo doesn't look surprised. 'I know,' he replies. 'That's the name Max said he wanted. ThunderButt!'

I can't believe it. He's painted 'ThunderButt' on the front of my superhero suit.

'I said Thunder*Bolt*!'

'What's a thunderbolt?' Hugo asks, scrunching up his face.

'In a storm!' I say.

'That's a *lightning* bolt! *Thunder* doesn't bolt,' Hugo says, which is actually quite a good point now that I think about it. 'I thought you said Thunder*Butt* as in, like, Kick*Butt*.'

'I actually don't mind it,' Tyson says. '*Thunder*Butt. Thunder*Butt*. Yeah, I can get used to that.'

'Well, you've painted it on now, so I guess it's ThunderButt, isn't it?' I say, putting on the superhero suit. 'How's it look?'

'Pretty good,' Tyson says.

'I totally can't tell it's you,' Hugo adds. He looks around the shed. 'Is this going to be our secret base?'

'Yeah, I figure it's important not to be too far away from the fridge if we need snacks,' I say, looking down at my costume.

* * * *

We spend the rest of Saturday designing the secret base, creating gadgets and coming up with the all-important origin story for ThunderButt.

We decide that ThunderButt, who can't have any actual superpowers because I don't have any (that I know of), needs to be one of the rich superheroes instead. You know, the ones who are awesome at fighting and forward rolls but other than that just use the fact that they are ridiculously rich to buy all the cool stuff they need.

So ThunderButt is the son of billionaire parents who became billionaires because they invented cheese that you can dunk biscuits into. Before them, there was only hard cheese which is impossible to dunk into. Anyway, unfortunately they died after being eaten by hippos (it turned out the earlier hippo conversation was rather helpful) while they were on safari. (His parents were on safari. Not the hippos.)

ThunderButt inherited billions of dollars, which he used to turn himself into a superhero to fight bad guys and homework. He's worked out the bad guys bit. He's still trying to solve the homework part. That's much harder.

Norman, his assistant (which is also the name of Captain Kickbutt's assistant, but that doesn't matter because no one ever knows the assistants' names anyway), is in charge of inventing gadgets. Luckily my dad invents lots of stuff in this shed so we're able to borrow some of that. Like this fishing rod with the electric motor on it. We can probably swing off buildings on that. Norman can test it.

'Norman, I think I need a car.'

'A real car?' Norman replies. He's busy at the moment trying to build me a parachute out of a doona cover. I'm busy resting on this beanbag.

'All superheroes have a vehicle.'

'But you can't drive.'

'We don't know that. I haven't tried,' I reply. 'Hey, where's Tyson? I haven't seen him for ages.'

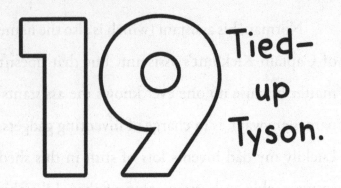

19 Tied-up Tyson.

So ThunderButt's first mission turns out to be a missing person's case and Tyson is the missing person! The Fridge must have kidnapped him.

Norman and I spend all of the afternoon running around Redhill trying to find him, or at least find a clue. To be honest though, I do most of the searching. Norman spends his time complaining about why, if he doesn't have a disguise, he has to change his name to Norman.

We're walking past an empty building site when I spot a clue. Tyson's black *SECURITY* cap.

I put my finger to my lips to signal Norman

to stop talking. He stops. Wow. I should have done that half an hour ago.

We tiptoe over to a half-constructed wall. It has a hole for a window but there's no glass in it. When we look through, we can see an unfinished staircase that leads down into what will probably be an underground garage. It's a big concrete basement.

That's not the interesting bit though. It's the fact that there are two chairs facing each other in the middle of the concrete floor. Tyson is tied to one of them. Across from him, pacing around the other chair, is the person who presumably tied him there: Abby Purcell.

Oh, I've seen this sort of thing on TV. Cops interview their suspect to try to find out if they did the crime. Abby must have read about it in one of her Hailey Plum books.

'I'm much more interested in where you were last Sunday morning,' Abby says.

'Lots of places,' Tyson replies.

'The jewellery store, perhaps?'

'You think I stole the necklace now?' Tyson asks.

I look at Hugo. I mean, Norman. This is getting ridiculous. Is Abby just working through my friends as her list of suspects? Abby keeps talking.

'I find it interesting that you want to be a bodyguard when you grow up and not a police officer,' she asks. 'Don't you want to be a police officer, Tyson?'

Tyson shakes his head. 'No.'

'Why not?' Abby asks.

'I don't like the uniform,' Tyson shrugs. 'It's blue. I don't like blue.'

'You're wearing blue pants, Tyson.'

He looks down. He must have forgotten about that. She's caught him out in a lie.

'I know the real reason you don't want to be a police officer,' Abby says. 'Cops have to care about right and wrong. Bodyguards don't necessarily need to worry about that. I was doing some investigating around the school. Answer me this, Tyson. Did you or did you not take half of Layla's honey sandwich last Thursday?'

'What?' Tyson screws up his face.

'It's a simple question, Tyson,' Abby glares. 'Did you steal her sandwich?'

'She'd finished it!' Tyson exclaims.

'That's not what she says, Tyson. She says you're a thief!' Abby is raising her voice now. 'And what about the case of Miss Sweet's missing lip balm?

'I did not steal Miss Sweet's lip balm!' Tyson's eyes open wide. 'That's crazy!'

'Is it, Tyson? Is it?' Abby pulls the lip balm out of her pocket!

He looks at it. 'That's not a lip balm. That's a glue stick. Isn't it?'

'Don't try and cover your tracks, Tyson. I'm onto you. Once a thief, always a thief!'

'I am not. I seriously thought that was a glue stick,' Tyson says.

Abby drops the glue stick and hops onto the other chair.

AND NOW YOU'VE STOLEN AGAIN, HAVEN'T YOU. DID YOU STEAL THE NECKLACE FROM GOLDSTEIN'S JEWELLERY?

'No!' Tyson says. 'I absolutely didn't. These are all silly coincidences!'

'Where's the necklace, Tyson?' Abby jumps to the ground, hands on her hips.

'I have no idea!' Tyson replies. 'I didn't steal it!'

'I don't believe you!' Abby yells.

'Untie me from this chair!'

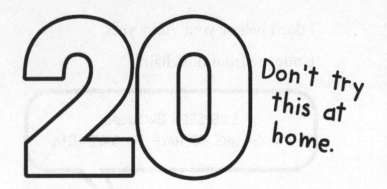

20

Don't try this at home.

Here we go. This is it. My first act as a superhero.

I just need to work out how to get down there. I can't use the staircase because it stops halfway down. I could run all the way around the other side of the building (it looks like there's a ramp on that side) but that wouldn't be very dramatic.

'I'll just jump through the window,' I whisper.

We both look through.

'That's a long way down,' whispers Hugo.

'It's what ThunderButt would do,' I say. I imagine all my favourite superheroes. Captain

Kickbutt is always jumping off towers and landing silently on the ground below. It never looks like it hurts. All right then. Here goes.

I jump.

I fall.

I ...

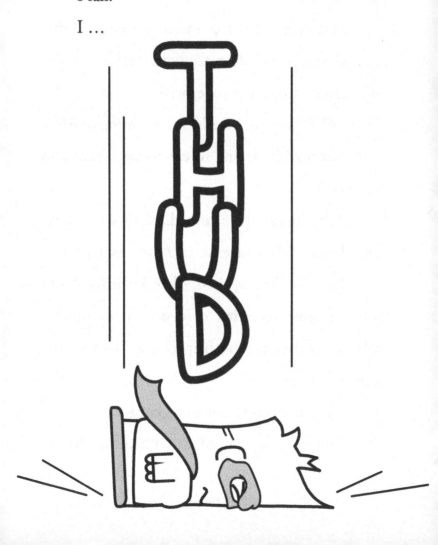

'Oof!' I land on my face right behind Abby. The cartoons were lying. That really hurt!

'Argh!' Abby screams. Apparently she wasn't expecting a costumed superhero to interrupt her little interrogation.

I clamber to my feet and remind myself that I need to use my deep Captain Kickbutt voice whenever I speak as a superhero.

'What have we here?' I say, pointing to Abby and Tyson while trying to catch my breath and not cry.

Abby looks a bit stunned. She looks me up and down. 'What have we … *here*?' she replies.

Tyson looks surprised. Then he grins. That's when I remember that of course Tyson knows who I am because he helped me 'borrow' the superhero suit.

'M–' he starts to say, but I cut him off.

'Son, you don't need to say another word.'

I turn to Abby. 'You, on the other hand, have a lot of explaining to do.'

Abby's not looking at my face. She's looking at my chest. 'Is ... is your name really ... *ThunderButt*?' she asks.

'I'll be asking the questions around here,' I reply, hands on my hips. 'Like, why do you have this gentleman tied to a chair?'

BECAUSE HE IS MY NUMBER ONE SUSPECT. I THINK HE MAY HAVE STOLEN THE NECKLACE FROM MR AND MRS GOLDSTEIN.

I look over at Tyson and then back at Abby. 'He didn't,' I say.

'Oh, really?' Abby puts her hands on her hips. 'How do you know that, ThunderButt?'

Good question. I don't know how I know. I just know. Let's go with that.

I JUST KNOW. IT'S ONE OF THE THINGS THAT I KNOW. I ALSO KNOW THAT YOU ARE NOT A REAL POLICE OFFICER, SO YOU'RE NOT ALLOWED TO KEEP PEOPLE LOCKED UP. YOU NEED TO LET HIM GO.

'Of course I'll let him go,' Abby says, rolling her eyes.

Victory. I walk around behind Tyson and pull the rope off him.

'Quick, kid!' I say. 'Run away. I have saved you.'

'You still have not explained why you think Tyson *didn't* steal the necklace!' Abby protests as Tyson wanders off.

'I told you. I can just tell. It's a hero thing,' I say. Superheroes speak deeply and in very short sentences. 'You don't have to worry about finding the thief any more, Abby. I'm here now. I'll do it. Good try though.'

Abby looks horrified. Then she looks mad. 'You don't get to tell me what to do, just because you're a kid in a costume!' she declares. 'I have never wanted to solve a mystery more in my entire life!'

'Don't be too hard on yourself, Abby Purcell. You're only human,' I reply. This is quite fun. 'Trust me, you're better off leaving crime fighting to the professionals.'

Abby looks like she's about to explode. Like, actually explode. Are her eyes glowing red?

I think I'd better get out of here. I'll follow

Tyson. He seemed to know the way.

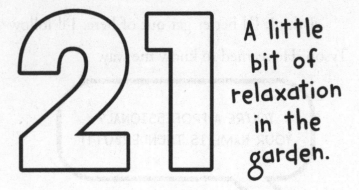

21
A little bit of relaxation in the garden.

The next morning, we're all at Pip and Tyson's house because Pip asked us to come and help with some gardening. That's right. She said 'gardening'.

Only 'gardening', it turns out, is a bit of an understatement.

Pip is constructing an entire floral display in her front yard dedicated to Spencer Daniels. Everyone will know it is dedicated to Spencer Daniels because the flowers spell out the words 'Spencer Daniels' across the front lawn.

'What can you possibly like about that twerp, Pip?' I ask.

'The heart wants what the heart wants, Max,'

Pip explains, which in my opinion doesn't explain anything at all. 'Every time I see him it makes my tummy flutter like it's full of butterflies.'

'Every time I see him, it makes my tummy flutter like it's full of cockroaches.'

'Max! Be nice!' Pip says. 'Let's change the subject.'

But you can't really change the subject when you're building an extravagant expression of love as a group activity. What am I supposed to do with these roses?

'Tyson, can you please pass me the shovel?' Abby asks.

'I'm not passing you anything,' Tyson snaps, glaring at her from behind a cracked love heart sign.

'What are you two fighting about?' Pip asks, carrying a handful of Christmas lights that she found in the attic. Apparently it's important that the sign is visible at night too.

'She thinks I stole the necklace from Hugo's parents!' Tyson explodes.

'Well, it wouldn't be the first time, would it?' Abby snaps back.

Pip hands Tyson some sticky tape. 'Please fix my broken heart,' she says. Then she turns to Hugo. 'When did you say the shop was robbed, Hugo?'

'The window was smashed at around eight o'clock last Sunday morning,' Hugo says.

'Well, then it can't have been Tyson,' Pip says to Abby, tying a bunch of flowers together and laying them down on the grass to form a giant 'S'.

'Why not?' Abby asks.

'Because he was with me,' she says. 'We were here having our traditional Sunday morning coffee with Dad. We do it every Sunday. Then he went to the newsagent's with Max and Hugo.'

'Aha, see! I have an alibi!' Tyson calls out. 'I forgot about that.'

Abby looks from twin to twin. 'Really, Pip?' she asks.

'Really,' Pip confirms and puts down a floral 'P' next to her floral 'S'.

Abby sits down on the grass. 'Well, this puts me right back at square one,' she says, pulling out her notebook and drawing a line through Tyson's name. 'If only we had that security camera footage! There must be something I'm missing!'

'There's something we're all missing,' I say. 'You guys drink coffee?'

Pip and Tyson look at each other.

'Only on Sundays.' Pip shrugs, adding an 'E'.

BUT YOU'RE ONLY ELEVEN!

22

ThunderButt saves your butt!

'It's okay, little guinea pig. You'll be fine up there. We'll get you down in just a minute.'

Oh, don't look at me like that. I know I just put a guinea pig in a tree, but it won't be for long. And it's all for a good cause. If I'm going to be a real superhero in Redhill, then I need to do real superhero things, like rescuing small children's pets when they get stuck in trees. I'm not big on heights myself, but look at him. He seems happy enough up there.

Okay. I need to hide.

I jump behind a bush and wait.

It doesn't take long.

I can hear Hugo's voice coming up the path.

'It's okay, little girl. I found your guinea pig,'
Hugo says. 'He's stuck in this tree.'

I peek out from behind the bush. Hugo is
walking towards me with the little girl who owns
the guinea pig. This is all going according to plan.

The little girl sees her guinea pig up in the
tree. 'Oh, no!' she says. 'Poor Nibbles!'

Hugo screws up his face. 'Your guinea pig is
called Nipples?'

The little girl looks horrified.

NIBBLES! NOT NIPPLES! CAN YOU GET HIM DOWN?

Hugo looks up into the tree and shakes his head. 'That's way too high for me,' he says, just like we planned. 'You know what we need in Redhill, little girl? Our own real hero. If only we had a –'

That's my cue.

I jump out of the bushes in full ThunderButt costume, my cape flapping in the wind.

'What seems to be the problem here?' I ask in my deep superhero voice.

'Argh!' the little girl screams. Why do people keep screaming every time I turn up? That never happens in *Captain Kickbutt* comics. No, they look really relieved and happy that a hero has turned up to save them. In Redhill, they look at me as though dressing up in a mask and a cape makes you some kind of weirdo. The girl asks, 'Who are you?'

'Oh, wow! That's ThunderButt!' Hugo says, just like we practised. 'I've heard about him. He's a real superhero!'

The little girl looks amazed. 'Wow! Can you fly?'

Why is that always the first question? It's presumptuous, that's what it is. As though you're only a real superhero if you can fly. Heaps of superheroes can't fly and, frankly, it's unfair to expect them to be able to! Cut us heroes some slack!

'Ah, no. Not really. But I can jump off stuff. And swing a bit,' I say.

She looks disappointed. See! Little kids these days have such high expectations! How about a little appreciation for the superhero that you do have, huh?

'Then how can you rescue Nibbles?' she asks, looking back up at her guinea pig.

Yeah. That's a fair question.

'Superheroes always have secret weapons and clever gadgets that they bring with them, little girl. ThunderButt is no different. I brought –' I reach back into the bush '– a stool.'

It's the same stool we used to put Nibbles up in the tree in the first place, so I know it works!

I pop the stool in front of the tree, climb up onto it without looking down and lift out the guinea pig.

'Thank you, ThunderButt!' says the little girl, running off.

'You're welcome!' I call after her. 'Go tell your friends that I saved Nibbles. And tell your parents about me. Your next door neighbours! Anyone you can!'

I turn to Hugo. I think that went well. 'We have to come up with a catchphrase for

ThunderButt,' I say. 'I need something to say when I burst out to save everyone.'

Hugo thinks for a bit. 'What about, "Holy Butt!"'

'Nah.' I shake my head. 'If I accidentally get that the wrong way round, I might end up yelling, "Butt Hole!" by mistake.'

'Not quite the impression you want to make.' Hugo nods. 'What about, "With a great butt comes great responsibility!"'

'Too long.' I shake my head.

'"Butts assemble?"' he suggests.

'Seriously?' I ask, imagining a whole line of butts. Ew. How terrifying.

'What about, "It's ThunderButt time!"'

'Yep, that's all right,' I admit. 'That'll do until we come up with something better.'

'It's ThunderButt time!' Hugo yells again.

'It's okay, Norman. You don't say it. I say it.'

NO, I MEAN IT'S THUNDERBUTT TIME RIGHT NOW! LOOK!

I look where he is pointing. On the other side of the park is a road and there's an old man trying to cross it. Only he's dropped his shopping bag right in the middle of the street and now he's chasing the rolling oranges around.

He hasn't seen the bus coming down towards him! And given that the bus doesn't seem to be slowing down, I don't think the bus driver has seen him either!

Hugo wasn't joking. It really is ThunderButt time!

I run across the park as fast as I can. I've never been very good at running, but now that I have this suit on, I feel like I can run faster than I've ever run before. My cape flaps in the wind behind me as I keep trying to go quicker and quicker.

I reach the road and the bus is still approaching. The old man, in his grey jumper, is actually quite hard to see on the grey road. He's so focused on those oranges, he hasn't seen the danger bearing down on him!

I do the only thing I can think to do. I leap onto the road in front of him. I hold out my hand towards the bus because that's what superheroes seem to do. (Even though it's really not going to do anything. I don't think I'm strong enough to stop a bus.) I yell:

STOP!

Maybe it is the flash of my bright yellow suit on the road. Maybe it is the red of my cape that's the same colour as a stop sign. Maybe I actually do have superpowers. Whatever it is, the driver sees me and slams on his brakes.

The bus screeches to a halt.

The old man looks up in surprise.

'It's ThunderButt time,' I whisper and realise that my heart is beating like crazy in my chest. I can't move. It all happened so quickly I didn't have time to be terrified, so weirdly I feel terrified now.

That's when I realise that on the side of the road and inside the bus there are people looking at me. They're taking photos with their phones. They're clapping. They're pointing and talking to each other.

I think I may have just become very famous.

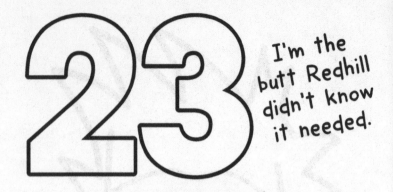

23

I'm the butt Redhill didn't know it needed.

'Miss Sweet! Did you see this?' It's Kevin calling out. He's opened the website for the *Redhill Daily* on a classroom computer and he's pointing to the headline.

We can all see it.

'HOLD ON TO YOUR THUNDERBUTT!'

There's a photo of me that someone on the bus took. You can't tell it's me, but everyone has been talking about it all morning.

'Yes, yes, I saw it,' says Miss Sweet. She's trying not to look impressed. I can tell.

'It's so cool!' Layla says. 'There's a real superhero kid in Redhill!'

DID YOU HEAR WHAT HE DID? HE SAVED THAT OLD MAN'S LIFE. SO EPIC!

HE SAVED ME TOO ONCE! FROM ABBY.

OH, SHHH! YOU WERE LOVING THE ATTENTION.

Of course, Tyson knows that I'm ThunderButt. So does Hugo. I'm not worried about that though. Those two can keep a secret. After all, they're my entourage.

'I heard he flew away,' Jade says. 'Did you hear that?'

'Oh, yeah. I saw him flying last night,' Tyson says. Okay, it seems he's quite enjoying this. 'He was a long way away, but it was definitely him.'

Abby looks at me. She squints. 'Max, did you see this kid?' she asks.

'Ah, yeah, sure,' I say. 'On TV last night. Seems like a pretty cool guy.'

I LIKE THE FACT THAT HE'S REAL. NOT LIKE ALL THESE ACTORS WHO ARE JUST PLAYING DRESS-UPS. I MEAN, WHAT HAS SPENCER DANIELS EVER ACTUALLY DONE TO HELP SOMEONE?

My point exactly. The thing is, everyone is nodding their heads. They agree! Wow, I think I might have just done it. I think I might be becoming more famous than Spencer Daniels!

HE'S DONE LOTS OF NICE THINGS FOR PEOPLE! WHEN HE FIRST ARRIVED IN REDHILL, HE WENT SHOPPING IN ALL THE LOCAL SHOPS AND BOUGHT PRESENTS FOR HIS MUM. DID YOU KNOW THAT?

I BET THAT WAS HIS MUM'S IDEA.

'He didn't buy anything when he visited my parents' shop,' Hugo says.

'Yeah, see? He's cheap!' I say.

'He is not cheap!' Pip yells at me.

'Woah, woah, woah,' Tyson says, squeezing in between Pip and me. 'Give Max some space, lady. I'm his bodyguard.'

'You're my brother,' Pip says and then whispers, 'And you know I could beat you up if I really wanted to.'

Tyson gulps.

'Spencer Daniels is doing a big press conference at the studio tomorrow afternoon,' Kevin reads, scrolling down the *Redhill Daily* website. 'There's a small article under the big story about ThunderButt. They'll be showing stuff from the movie and everything. We should all go.'

Everyone crowds around the computer to read about it. But I've heard all that I needed to hear: 'Small article under the big story about ThunderButt.'

Take that, Famous Kid.

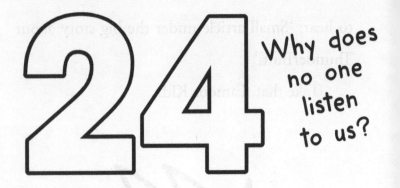

24 Why does no one listen to us?

The bell goes and it's the end of another day at school. Boy, they work us hard in that place. We had to do Maths, Science and English all in the same day. Then Miss Sweet wanted to tell us about something that happened a long time ago and she expected us to try to remember it!

It's not all about school, you know! We've got more going on in our lives. Like being superheroes. Solving robberies. Telling famous people that we love them! (That last one was Pip, just in case anyone was confused.)

'Does anyone want to come with me to see

Spencer Daniels?' Pip asks as we step out of the school gate.

'The big press conference isn't until tomorrow afternoon, Pip,' Tyson reminds her.

'Oh, I know. But I want to invite him over to our house so that he can see the garden,' she says with a big smile. I've seen the finished garden. It's impressive and slightly terrifying all at the same time. Pip is still grinning and nodding. 'He needs to see the garden.'

Tyson throws his hands in the air in frustration, almost knocking his *SECURITY* cap off his head. 'This is exactly why famous people need bodyguards like me and The Fridge!' he exclaims. 'Because of people like you who think they can just go and harass them whenever they feel like it.'

'I'm not harassing him, Tyson,' Pip says, crossing her arms. 'I just built him a love garden. It's perfectly normal.'

'It's not!' Tyson yells, so frustrated that he runs out of words. He tries again. 'You can't …!'

Nope. He ran out of words again.

Pip isn't impressed. She turns to Abby. 'Will you come with me?' Pip asks.

'Can't,' Abby replies. She's been ignoring most of this so far, scribbling something in her notebook instead. 'I have to go and ask Mr and Mrs Goldstein some more questions.'

Hugo's ears prick up. 'What?' Hugo asks with a frown. 'Why, Abby?'

Now it's Hugo's turn to throw his hands in the air. 'No, you can't!' he exclaims. 'Leave my parents alone. They've been through enough without you bothering them!'

Abby looks at him, confused. She looks at Tyson in the same way. 'There's one thing you boys seem to be forgetting,' she says.

'What's that?' Tyson and Hugo ask at the same time.

Abby grins and nods at Pip.

And with that Abby turns and walks left, Pip turns and walks right, and we three boys stand there trying to work out why no one listens to us.

Tyson turns to Hugo and me. There's an urgency in his voice. 'We've got to stop Pip,' he says. 'If I can stop her, then maybe The Fridge will like me again.'

'Why do you care so much about whether The Fridge likes you?' I ask.

'Because I can't stand this feeling that I've disappointed him,' Tyson says. 'He's my hero!'

'You seem as obsessed with him as Pip is with Famous Kid,' I say.

'That's not true. I haven't built him a love garden,' Tyson says and then adds, 'yet.'

'No, you've got to stop Abby,' Hugo protests. 'She keeps coming up with these crazy theories and annoying my parents. Tyson, you're my bodyguard too, remember? You've got to stop Abby!'

'I can't! There are too many girls to stop!' Tyson yells and then turns to me. 'Max, I have to stop my sister. Can ThunderButt help Hugo stop Abby?'

'Ah,' I say. 'I dunno, you'd have to ask ThunderButt.'

MAX! WE KNOW, REMEMBER?

OH, YEAH. OF COURSE. SORRY, IT'S HARD WORK SPENDING ALL DAY TRYING TO NOT BE A SUPERHERO.

Frankly I don't know how Peter Parker does it. It's exhausting.

I am keen for a bit more superhero action though. This running-around-with-a-cape-and-getting-famous thing is kinda fun.

THAT SOUNDS LIKE A GOOD PLAN. LET'S SPLIT UP TO STOP THE GIRLS FROM RUINING THE WORLD WITH ALL THEIR LOVE AND JUSTICE. IT'S THUNDERBUTT TIME!

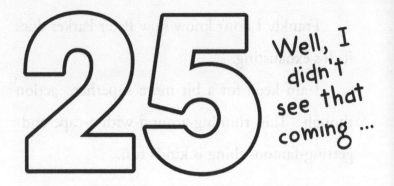

Well, I didn't see that coming ...

When Hugo and I arrive at his parents' jewellery store, Abby is already inside. Hugo seems frustrated at being late, but it took me a while to get my costume on. I know Superman can somehow whip his on in a phone booth, but it's actually quite tricky to get all that lycra on without giving yourself a wedgie.

Hugo takes me around the side of the store so we can enter through the back door. As soon as we come into the storeroom area, we can hear Abby talking to his parents in the front.

'Do you have any idea who robbed your store, Mr and Mrs Goldstein?' Abby asks.

'We don't,' Hugo's mum replies. 'If only we had the security camera footage, we would be able to see who smashed the window and took the necklace off the display counter.'

We peek through the curtain that divides the storeroom from the shopfront. There are customers in the shop and Mr and Mrs Goldstein are trying to serve them while Abby buzzes around.

'So it was right here?' Abby asks, pointing to a display box on one of the counters.

Hugo's dad looks over from where he's talking to a customer. He looks mildly irritated.

YES, BUT LOOK, YOUR MUM, SERGEANT PURCELL, SEEMS TO HAVE EVERYTHING UNDER CONTROL, SO WHY DON'T ...

'And when was the security camera cable cut again?' Abby interrupts, writing something down in her notebook.

If there's one thing I can relate to here, it's finding Abby Purcell super annoying. Welcome to my life, Mr and Mrs Goldstein!

ABOUT 4:30 ON SATURDAY AFTERNOON. WE WOULD HAVE BEEN IN THE STORE WHEN IT HAPPENED. THE CABLE WAS CUT AROUND THE BACK. BUT LOOK, WE'VE TOLD ALL THIS TO THE POLICE ...

Hugo elbows me in the ribs. Okay, okay.

I step out from behind the curtain in my full ThunderButt costume and stand there with my hands on my hips. 'Abby Purcell, I think that's quite enough,' I announce to the shop.

Everyone freezes. The customers look at me,

look at Mr and Mrs Goldstein, look at Abby. Abby rolls her eyes. Hugo's parents look mostly confused.

Then Mr Goldstein steps towards us. He suddenly looks like he's worked out what's going on. 'Oh, you're that superhero kid from the newspaper,' he says. He turns from me to Abby.

RIGHT, WELL, IF YOU KIDS COULD ALL GO AND PLAY SOMEWHERE ELSE, WE'RE TRYING TO SELL JEWELLERY IN HERE. I'M SURE YOU UNDERSTAND.

THUNDER BUTT

He gives us a big grin, which looks incredibly fake. He clearly doesn't realise that I'm on his side in all of this.

'That's exactly what I was about to say, Mr Goldstein,' I continue. 'Abby, you need to leave these poor people alone.'

Abby closes her notebook and glares at me.

ONE MORE QUESTION THOUGH. DID YOU SEE THE NECKLACE WHEN YOU CLOSED THE SHOP AT 5 P.M. ON SATURDAY AFTERNOON?

Somehow I still get surprised with just how irritating Abby Purcell can be. How is that even possible?

'Abby, I said that's enough.' I make my superhero voice extra deep.

She ignores me extra hard. 'Mr and Mrs Goldstein,' she asks again, with more urgency this time. She clearly wants an answer to this question before she's kicked out of here.

> DID YOU DEFINITELY SEE THE NECKLACE ON THE COUNTER WHEN YOU CLOSED THE STORE?

'Well, ah, I assume it was there,' Mrs Goldstein says, but she doesn't seem sure. 'It's always there.'

'But did you actually see it?' Abby asks.

I realise I haven't really being paying attention to what Abby is asking them. Why does she want to know if the necklace was on the counter when they closed the shop the day before the robbery?

'I don't … remember,' Mr Goldstein admits, looking over at his wife. She shrugs as though they've never thought about it before.

That's when Hugo steps out from behind the curtain. Even he wants to know what's going on now.

WHAT ARE YOU THINKING, ABBY?

THAT WE'VE BEEN LOOKING AT THIS ALL WRONG. WE'VE BEEN ASSUMING THAT THE WINDOW WAS SMASHED WHEN THE NECKLACE WAS STOLEN. BUT WHAT IF THE WINDOW WAS JUST MEANT TO DISTRACT US?

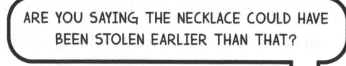

ARE YOU SAYING THE NECKLACE COULD HAVE BEEN STOLEN EARLIER THAN THAT?

BEFORE YOU CLOSED ON SATURDAY AFTERNOON, IN FACT. SOMETIME BETWEEN 4:30 WHEN THE SECURITY CAMERA CABLE WAS CUT AND FIVE O'CLOCK WHEN YOU CLOSED.

THAT WOULD MEAN THE THIEF WAS IN THE STORE WITH US? LIKE A CUSTOMER?

'They slipped it into a bag or pocket while you were distracted and then they simply smashed the window the next morning to make it look like your store had been broken into,' Abby says.

Who cares? Why does it matter whether the necklace was stolen on Saturday afternoon or Sunday morning? This is getting ridiculous.

Plus, everyone here seems to have forgotten about me. Surely the most interesting thing right now is that there's a real-life superhero in the shop?

I step forward. 'This doesn't make any sense,' I say. 'Come on, Abby. Let's go.'

Abby looks straight past me at Mr and Mrs Goldstein.

'Actually … it does make sense,' Hugo's dad says.

It does?

'Do you remember who was in the store after 4:30 on Saturday afternoon?' Abby asks.

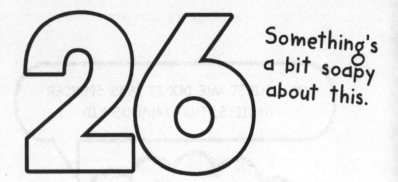

26

Something's a bit soapy about this.

'We've solved it. Famous Kid stole the necklace!'
I say in my excited ThunderButt voice. We've just
left Hugo's parents' shop and we're standing out in
the street. Mr and Mrs Goldstein said they would
talk to Abby's mum about Abby's theory, but I
don't see why we have to wait for that to happen.
I'm finally going to get to beat Famous Kid once
and for all. 'Let's take him to jail. We've got him!'

'No, we don't,' Abby replies, still scribbling
in her notebook.

'What do you mean, we don't?' I ask. I've
watched enough *Captain Kickbutt* cartoons and
read enough *Captain Kickbutt* comics to know

how it works. Find the bad guy, then catch the bad guy.

'We have a suspect,' Abby says. 'But we don't have any *proof*.'

Oh, come on! She must be getting this stuff from her Hailey Plum books. *Proof?*

WHY DO WE NEED PROOF? ISN'T IT OBVIOUS HE DID IT?

Abby sighs the same way Miss Sweet often closes a textbook and sighs. It's a sigh that seems to say, 'How did I get lumped with you lot?'

'What are you going to say?' Abby asks. 'What are you going to do? Walk up to him and

say, "Spencer Daniels, you stole a necklace!"?
He'll just say, "No, I didn't." And then you'll be
like … Oh, what now?'

I really thought she would be more friendly
to ThunderButt than she is to me, but no,
apparently not.

I WOULDN'T SAY THAT, I'D SAY, 'IT'S
THUNDERBUTT TIME!' THAT'S WHAT I'D SAY.
MAX WALBURT MIGHT SAY THAT OTHER
STUFF. BY THE WAY, WHERE IS THE FUNNY
KID? I MISS MAX. HE'S THE BEST.

I turn around everywhere, pretending to look for Max. Abby stares at me strangely.

Luckily Pip and Tyson turn up, although Pip looks really sad and Tyson ... well, Tyson has soap suds coming out of his ears. How could they go and visit Spencer Daniels at his trailer and end up looking like this?

WHAT HAPPENED, PIP? WHAT'S WRONG?

Really, Hugo? Surely the obvious first question should be about the soap suds?

SPENCER DANIELS WAS AWFUL!

I grin. I think that might be my favourite sentence of all time.

'What did he do?' Abby asks.

'Well, I got to his trailer and knocked on the door, and his mum came out,' Pip says. Famous Kid's mum always seems to be lurking around in the shadow of his giant head. She's kinda creepy. 'I said I wanted to see Spencer, and she called me a little rat and told me to go away!'

'She called you a rat?' Hugo asks, surprised.

'It gets worse,' Tyson says. This must be the soap suds bit. 'I told her she wasn't allowed to speak to my sister that way. That, actually, Pip had done something really nice for Spencer, even if it was a little bit, you know … weird, and that she just wanted to tell him about it.'

No soap suds yet.

'That's when The Fridge came out,' Pip says. 'He had this big plastic bucket in his hand.

He'd been washing up. There were soap suds and stuff.'

Okay, there are the suds, but how did they get on Tyson? This is turning into a really long story.

'I was like, okay, cool, this guy will understand,' Tyson says. 'The Fridge is my mentor. We have a connection, you know?'

ANYWAY, SPENCER CALLS OUT FROM INSIDE THE TRAILER ASKING WHO WAS THERE. SPENCER'S MUM GOES, 'OH, THEY'RE JUST DIRTY NOT-FAMOUS PEOPLE.' AND THEN SHE TELLS THE FRIDGE TO GET RID OF US!

Hugo puts his hand over his mouth in astonishment. 'This is horrible,' he says.

I KNOW! UNBELIEVABLE! IT'S A SHAME MAX ISN'T AROUND TO HEAR THIS.

Pip screws up her face and looks at me weirdly.

SO I SAY TO THE FRIDGE, 'LISTEN HERE, PAL. THERE'S NO NEED FOR THIS TO GET UGLY. WE UNDERSTAND EACH OTHER. WE'RE BOTH BODYGUARDS AND SURELY YOU CAN SEE THAT PIP JUST WANTS TO TALK TO SPENCER AND SURELY THAT'S NOT A BIG DEAL, RIGHT? BODYGUARD TO BODYGUARD?'

'You'll never believe what he did,' Pip says.

'What?' Abby, Hugo and I reply together.

Surely this is the important bit.

HE TIPPED THE DIRTY WASHING-UP WATER ALL OVER TYSON!

Thank you! This is why Tyson has

soap suds in his ears. Finally.

HE JUST TOOK THE WHOLE BUCKET AND FLIPPED IT OVER, AND TYSON GOT COVERED IN DIRTY WATER AND SOAP SUDS. SO I WAS LIKE, 'YOU CAN'T DO THAT, YOU MONSTER! MY BROTHER IDOLISES YOU. HE THINKS YOU'RE SO COOL. YOU NEED TO TREAT HIM WITH RESPECT!'

I DIDN'T HEAR MOST OF THAT, BECAUSE I HAD SOAP SUDS IN MY EARS.

'Then out comes Spencer finally. He's like, "What's going on out here?" and then he sees Tyson and he starts laughing,' Pip says. 'He goes, "Aren't you George Khan's kids?" and I'm thinking, oh, good, he's going to apologise for his insane mum and his kitchen-appliance bodyguard. So I'm like, "Yeah," and then he goes, "I hate your dad!" He said he was a bad actor and he was ugly! In fact, we're all ugly and Redhill stinks and he can't wait to get out of this stupid place!'

'What a horrible person!' Abby says.

'I know,' I add, shaking my head. 'Max would be horrified!'

They seem to have stopped noticing that I keep saying my own name all the time. That's good. I don't think they have any idea that Max Walburt and ThunderButt are actually the same person.

'He turned out to be the most awful person I've ever met!' Pip says.

'No one is allowed to speak to my friends like that!' Hugo says, putting his hands on his hips. 'Or pour dirty soap suds on them!'

'He's not just awful,' I say, using my deep ThunderButt voice. I turn to Pip and Hugo. 'He's also a thief. He stole the necklace from the Goldsteins. We just worked it out.'

The twins gasp.

'Oh, *we* did, did *we*?' Abby says, glaring at me.

She's not much of a team player, that Abby Purcell.

'No way!' Pip says. 'Really?'

'We think he did,' Abby replies. 'We just need proof.'

I cross my arms and scowl. She's on about *proof* again.

'I want to get this guy so bad,' I say. 'I bet Max would want to get him too.'

Everyone gives me that weird look again.

'So how do we get proof?' Hugo asks Abby.

'Either we find some evidence that shows that he did it,' Abby explains, 'or we find a way to get him to admit to it.'

Now, that's an interesting idea. I had been imagining we were going to have to do something really boring like dusting for fingerprints or talking to witnesses or yawn, yawn, yawn. But, instead, what if we could do a sort of 'sting'? A face-off between ThunderButt and Famous Kid? A face-off where Famous Kid goes down!

'How would we ever get him to admit to it?' Pip asks, but my mind is already racing.

'He's got this big press conference tomorrow, right?' I ask in my deep, confident ThunderButt voice.

'Yeah,' Tyson says.

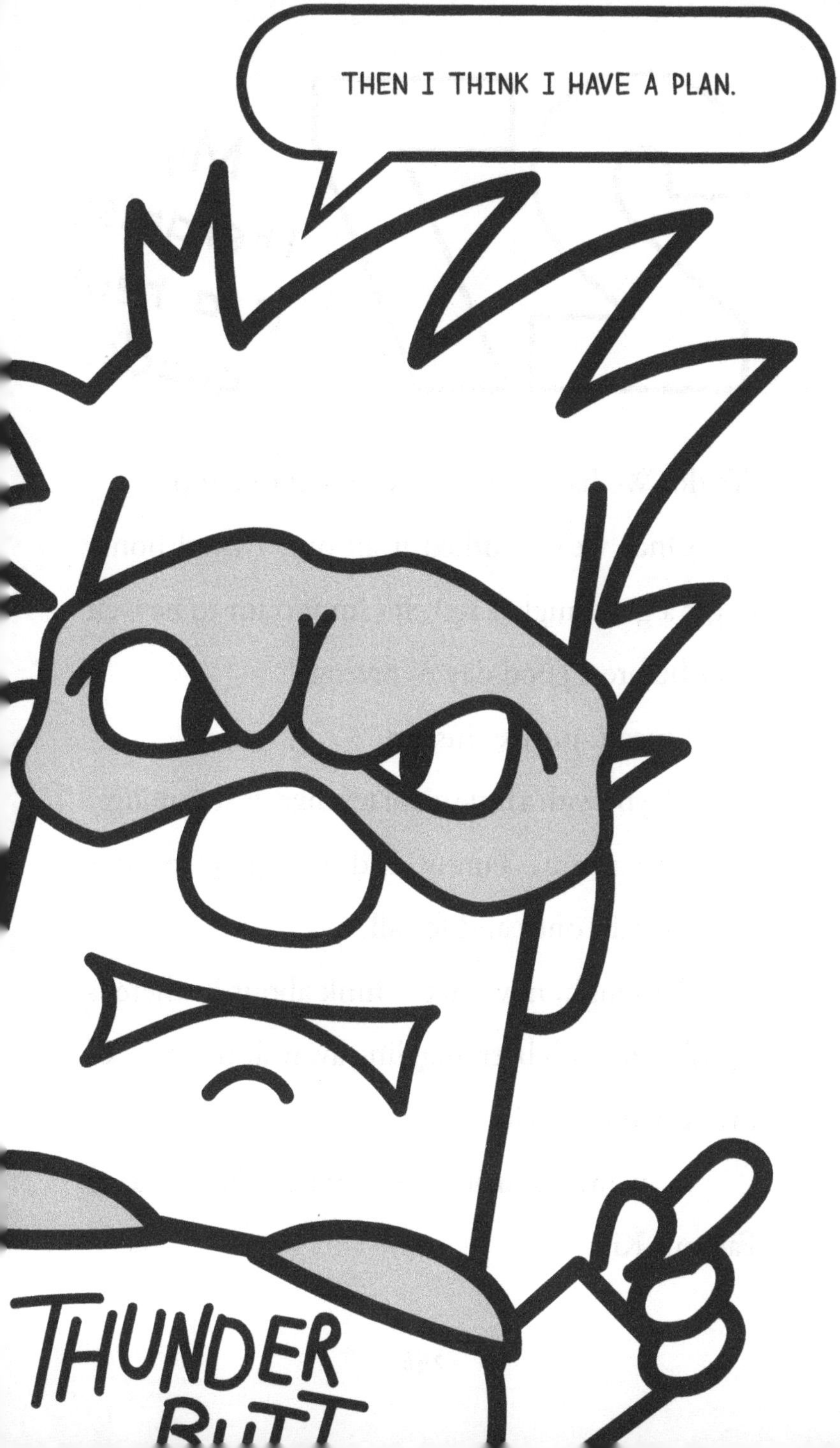
THEN I THINK I HAVE A PLAN.
THUNDER BUTT

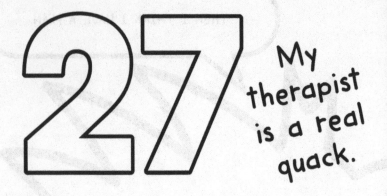

27 My therapist is a real quack.

We do. We have a plan. It's a good one too.

Once we've worked it all out, I head home to get a good night's rest. It's important to be well slept before a good day of revenge.

I mean, justice. Justice.

Maybe with a little bit of revenge. Just a smidge.

Either way, Funny Kid is going to beat Famous Kid once and for all.

Although, now that I think about it, there is a problem that's been niggling away at the back of my very busy brain.

It won't actually be Funny Kid beating Famous Kid.

It will be ThunderButt beating Famous Kid.

I'm beginning to realise there's a problem with this whole superhero thing. I hadn't noticed it until I became an actual hero.

You don't actually become famous. Your superhero does.

See, the only reason I became a superhero was to become more famous than Spencer Daniels. Only Peter Parker isn't that famous. Spider-Man is. And no one in Metropolis cares about Clark Kent. Superman is the star.

What good is it if I beat Famous Kid, but nobody knows it was me?

Somewhere along the way I've made a mistake. This was not the plan.

Quack!

I turn around. Duck is standing behind me. My feathered friend always knows how to find me when I'm stuck. He nods towards a nearby park bench.

'You want me to sit on the bench?' I ask.

Duck nods.

Ah, okay. I sit on the park bench.

Duck quacks and tilts his head to the side.

'You want me to lie down?' Duck nods. 'I don't want to lie down.'

Duck glares at me. Okay, okay. Most of the time it's just easier to do what the bird says. He can get in such a huff when he doesn't get his own way.

Duck hops up on the park bench at the other end, sits down and looks at me as if to say, 'Tell me all your problems.'

Gladly.

ALL I WANTED WAS TO BE A MASSIVE CELEBRITY, DUCK. IS THAT TOO MUCH TO ASK?

I look up into the sky just as a cloud goes by that makes me think of cheeseballs.

Quack! That's duck language for 'Focus, Max! Focus!'

'I've even succeeded at becoming famous. ThunderButt is everywhere! He's on the TV, he's in the newspapers. All the kids at school are talking about him. But they don't know that it's me!'

Quack! That's what Duck says when he wants to say, 'It sounds like you're jealous of the made-up superhero you invented.'

'Well ... yes, I guess when you put it like that, I am,' I admit. 'I don't just have to compete with Famous Kid. I'm having to compete with ThunderButt as well, even though I created ThunderButt!'

Quack! Which in this case means, 'Well ... Hugo was also involv–'

'Shhh! Duck, that's unhelpful.'

Duck rolls his eyes. So much attitude. He jumps off the park bench and starts to act something out. He puts his wings over his face, covering his eyes and then slowly lifts them up and over his head.

'Peepo?' I guess.

Duck does it again. Wings over his face and lifts them up over his head. Almost like he's taking off a mask. Ohhh, I get it. You know what? That's not such a bad idea.

'Do you mean, it's time to take off my mask and show everyone that I am ThunderButt?'

Duck does a slow nod.

Superheroes never do that. They spend their whole time trying *not* to take off the mask. They're always wanting to make sure people *don't* find out their real identity. But then, I guess, they're not really trying to get famous.

'If I revealed that I was the real hero, then I could become famous instead of ThunderButt! But I'd need to do it in front of a lot of people ...' I say, trying to think. And then, 'Of course! That's it! The press conference! It's the perfect moment.'

Duck rolls his eyes as if to say he thought of that five minutes ago.

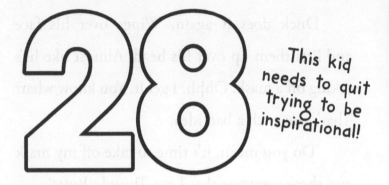

28

This kid needs to quit trying to be inspirational!

The press conference is at the *Captain Kickbutt* studio in one of the big old warehouse rooms. I guess this room was full of chicken soup cans once upon a time. Now it's filled with half the town of Redhill and journalists from the TV and newspapers. They're all looking up at a stage where Rhonda Anderson Delaney, Spencer Daniels, George Khan and Parakeet are sitting and answering questions.

As for me? I'm hiding behind the stage dressed as ThunderButt. Hugo is with me. Tyson, full of motivation again, is watching out for

The Fridge or Parakeet or whoever else might want to disrupt our plan. Out in the crowd, Abby and Pip are sitting, ready for their part in taking down ThunderButt's evil nemesis, Famous Kid.

If the plan works, I'm going to reveal ThunderButt's true identity to the world. But I'm keeping that to myself for now.

SOME OF THE SPECIAL EFFECTS WE'RE USING IN THIS FILM HAVE NEVER BEEN SEEN BEFORE. YOU'LL REALLY BELIEVE A YOUNG BOY CAN KICK BUTT.

'And what do you say to criticism that the *Captain Kickbutt* movie is going to be too dark and serious?' asks a journalist.

The director takes a breath. 'There's nothing funny about fighting for truth and justice in a dying world,' she says gloomily.

Really? But they're doing it in tights and a cape, RAD. And his name's Kickbutt. She's missing the whole point. It's supposed to be funny!

'Spencer, have you always been a fan of the *Captain Kickbutt* comics?' another journalist asks.

'Of course,' Famous Kid replies. 'I've always loved Captain Kickbutt and Hammerhead and … Nelson.'

I turn to Hugo, horrified. Nelson? *Nelson?*

'It's *NORMAN*!' I hiss.

'I know!' Hugo hisses back. And he does. He really does.

I knew it! Famous Kid isn't even a Captain Kickbutt fan.

'Spencer, I assume you've heard about the kid in the costume who stopped the bus on the weekend?' another reporter asks.

Oh, this should be good. They're talking about me!

'Do you feel a sense of pride knowing that you've inspired the children of Redhill, and the world, to do the right thing?'

I'm sorry. *What?* Inspired by Spencer Daniels? You've got to be joking.

DEFINITELY. I TAKE MY RESPONSIBILITY AS A ROLE MODEL VERY SERIOUSLY.

Oh, I've never wanted to thump somebody so bad! Is he really taking credit for ThunderButt? He better not be taking credit for ThunderButt!

Spencer Daniels continues, 'To think that I've been able to inspire a kid to want to be like me by caring for the elderly –'

Oh, I've had about enough of this.

Come on, Abby and Pip. Let's get this show started.

29 Teddy bear love.

'Let's have the next question from a member of the public,' says the host of the press conference. 'How about you there? The blonde girl with her hand up?'

Pip stands up in the crowd and someone hands her a microphone.

Okay. Here we go.

HI, SPENCER. WHAT'S IT LIKE BEING FAMOUS?

Of course, after yesterday's incident at the trailer, Pip now hates Spencer Daniels' guts. For our plan to work, though, Pip has to pretend that she's still hopelessly in love. She's doing a good job too.

'It's ... ah, it's pretty sweet,' Spencer Daniels replies.

AND CAN YOU DO WHATEVER YOU WANT?

'Of course I can,' Famous Kid answers.

From where I'm sitting, I can see Abby next to Pip, scribbling questions on little bits of paper and passing them to her. Pip quickly reads the next one.

DO YOU EVER GET IN TROUBLE FOR ANYTHING?

'Of course not. Can you imagine a face as cute as mine ever getting in trouble?'

Ugh. Gross.

'So you can just have anything you want all the time and you never get in trouble? That's so cool,' Pip gushes. She reads the next question that Abby passes her. 'And what's your favourite thing that you own?'

That's it! That's our cue!

I look at Hugo and nod. He reaches over to the sound system behind the stage and turns down the volume on Spencer Daniels' microphone. At the same time, he turns up the volume of the one that we plugged in earlier. It's just like the prank I did at school, only with a much bigger audience.

I put on my best Spencer Daniels voice and answer Pip's question. 'My teddy. My teddy is my favourite thing.'

The audience chuckles. Famous Kid taps his microphone to see if it's working. I tap mine in time so that it makes the right noise.

Spencer tries to speak into his microphone again, trying to tell everyone that it's not working. Instead I keep talking in my Famous Kid voice.

I LOVE MY TEDDY. HE'S SO SOFT AND SQUISHY, AND HE MAKES ME FEEL ALL WARM INSIDE.

I see Spencer's whole body tense up. He starts looking around frantically. He seems furious that this is happening to him again.

And this time the audience is finding it quite entertaining.

As planned, Pip quickly moves onto the next question. 'Spencer, do you ever give your teddy … presents?'

Famous Kid is getting mad now and jumps off his chair. He yells into his microphone, but no one can hear him because I speak through my working microphone at the same time.

OH, YES. I LOVE GIVING TEDDY PRESENTS.

Spencer Daniels starts shaking his fists in the air while the crowd bursts into fits of laughter.

That's when I hear a growl. I look to my left.

Uh-oh.

The Fridge!

He's turned up behind the stage and he's only looking for one person. Me. His muscles are flexing. His shoulders are tense and he looks about ten degrees icier than normal.

He spots Hugo and me over by the sound system, and suddenly he's barrelling towards us, just like that bus was charging towards me a few days ago.

I hold out my hand, but even I'm not sure it's going to work twice.

The problem is, I need to keep talking into the microphone. We haven't got Famous Kid to admit to stealing the necklace yet. We need more time! If The Fridge stops us now, it's all over!

I hold tight to the microphone and brace myself for impact. Hugo and I are about to get pulverised.

STOP RIGHT THERE!

SECURITY

It's Tyson! From out of nowhere, he's jumped in front of Hugo and me, and he's pointing his finger directly at The Fridge. Famous Kid's bodyguard halts in surprise.

'You leave my friends alone!' Tyson says fiercely. The Fridge looks a little stunned, but Tyson isn't done.

YOU CALL YOURSELF A BODYGUARD, BUT YOU'RE JUST A BULLY. I LOOKED UP TO YOU. I THOUGHT YOU WERE THE BEST, BUT YOU TURNED OUT TO BE JUST AS NASTY AS THAT BRAT OF A KID YOU'RE LOOKING AFTER. AND HIS CRAZY MOTHER! I'M DISAPPOINTED IN YOU, FRIDGE. YOU ARE A DISAPPOINTING FRIDGE!

Woah.

The Fridge sits down on his bum.

The Fridge gets a wobbly bottom lip.

The Fridge starts to cry.

Tyson looks over at Hugo and me as if to say, 'Oops. Now what do I do?' He reaches out and puts his hand on The Fridge's shoulder. 'There, there, Mr Fridge. It's all right.'

This is all very touching, but I'm in the middle of a prank on Spencer Daniels that's supposed to get him to confess. I don't have time for all this emotion.

I turn back to the stage where Famous Kid is banging the microphone on the floor and trying to get it to work. That's when Rhonda Anderson Delaney comes over to him and hands him *her* microphone!

'Uh-oh,' I whisper. 'Quick, Hugo!'

Famous Kid lifts it to his mouth to speak just as Hugo works out which volume control is the director's and turns down her volume too. I speak into my microphone using my best Spencer Daniels voice.

'I give teddy lots of presents. Teddy gets whatever teddy wants.'

Famous Kid starts jumping up and down on the spot like a two-year-old. I keep going.

'Teddy has very expensive taste. He likes limousines and … jewellery.'

JEWELLERY?

I answer quickly, 'Oh, yes. Earrings. Bracelets … Necklaces.'

Famous Kid is throwing a full-on tantrum now and the camera flashes from the news photographers are going crazy. He grabs a microphone off George Khan and tries to use that, but Hugo flicks the volume down just in time.

'In fact, I got my teddy his very own necklace,' I say. 'It's so beautiful. It's got a gold chain with this beautiful diamond in the middle and the diamond is made up of lots of other diamonds. I wish you could all see it.'

That's Abby's cue. She leaps to her feet and grabs the microphone from Pip. As she does, she holds up a picture of the Goldsteins' stolen necklace.

'Is it this necklace, Spencer Daniels?'

Suddenly the whole swarm of reporters turns towards Abby to see the picture she's holding up. They all recognise it, of course, because it's been all over the newspapers for a week.

YES! THAT'S THE ONE. I TOOK IT FOR MY TEDDY BECAUSE HE LOVES ME AND I LOVE HIM!

THUNDER BUTT

Famous Kid spins around and glares towards the back of the stage. He knows we're back here somewhere. He must be wondering why The Fridge hasn't been able to stop us. Turns out we have Tyson, the best bodyguard in the world.

Spencer Daniels picks up his stool and throws it at the back curtain of the stage as though that's going to stop us. The crowd gasps in shock.

'Sometimes I act like a big superstar,' I say. 'But actually what I really want to do right now is go home and snuggle with my teddy.'

Famous Kid turns back around to the crowd and tries to yell something into the microphone. No one hears it. Instead they hear me saying:

'Teddy! Teddy! I stole a necklace for you!'

I can see from the way Spencer Daniels' tantrum has reached full throttle that he's had enough. I turn to Hugo. 'Quick! Turn the volume on his microphone back up!'

Hugo flicks it and suddenly, louder than ever, we hear the real Spencer Daniels cry:

I DIDN'T STEAL THE NECKLACE FOR MY TEDDY! I STOLE IT FOR MY MUMMY!

The whole room goes silent.

We did it. We got him. He just confessed.

Click. Click. Click.

That's the sound of the cameras in the press conference starting to go crazy again.

Famous Kid just admitted to being a thief.

I can't quite believe that it worked.

Now is my moment. I put down the microphone. I jump up onto the stage and step through the curtain in front of the crowd of cameras.

I see Abby and Pip looking at me, happy but also confused. We didn't talk about ThunderButt getting onto the stage at the end.

I look to the side of the stage where Sergeant Purcell and another police officer are walking up to arrest Spencer Daniels. On the other side of the stage, there are more police officers who have surrounded Famous Kid's mummy. She's throwing an enormous tantrum. That's embarrassing.

I stand right in the centre of it all, fists on my hips, chest thrust out, a gentle breeze from somewhere blowing my cape out behind me.

What a moment to be a hero!

I reach my hand up, ready to pull off my mask and reveal that ThunderButt is actually Redhill's one and only Funny Kid …

… when suddenly Rhonda Anderson Delaney calls out:

HEY! I KNOW THAT COSTUME! THAT'S FROM MY COSTUME DEPARTMENT! YOU STOLE THAT COSTUME FROM MY MOVIE SET!

Gulp.

Oh, yeah. I forgot about that.

Suddenly all eyes are on me. The reporters and photographers. The crowd of onlookers from Redhill. The kids from school. All the people making the movie.

And the police.

I've just busted a thief while wearing a *stolen* costume!

Eek. Maybe pulling off my mask right now is not such a good idea, after all?

I think I need a change of plan.

Yep, my plan is now … RUN AWAY!

31 Hanging up my cape.

Luckily for me, the police were more interested in a piece of expensive stolen jewellery than they were in the fact that I'd borrowed a costume and forgotten to give it back. I managed to get away from the press conference and get home, then spent the rest of the night going through all the cleaning products in our house to remove 'ThunderButt' from the superhero suit.

Then this morning I snuck out early and went via the film studio on the way to school to sneak into the costume department and return the costume.

As I hang it back on a clothing rack, I give it one last pat. 'Goodbye, ThunderButt,' I whisper.

'Even though Redhill will never know that you and I were the same person, it's still been fun.'

I slip back out of the costume department, jog across the parking lot and head towards the street.

Which is where I find Abby, Hugo, Pip, Tyson and Duck all waiting for me.

WHAT ARE YOU GUYS DOING HERE?

'What were *you* doing here, Max?' Abby asks, raising one eyebrow.

'Oh … um, well …'

Quick. I need a good cover story.

Suddenly Abby starts to laugh. The others quickly join in.

'We're just messing with you, Max,' Abby says. 'We knew you were ThunderButt the whole time.'

'What? Really?'

'Of course! Everyone did!' Pip says, laughing. 'It was so obvious!'

'You superhero kids,' Abby says, shaking her head as we start to walk to school. 'You think you can just pop a mask on your face and speak in a stupid voice and nobody will recognise you. I tell you who doesn't wear a mask, Max: Hailey Plum!'

'Oh, would you stop going on about Hailey Plum?' I say.

'Hey, Max, now that Spencer Daniels has been fired from the movie, they need to cast someone new as young Captain Kickbutt,' Tyson says. 'Do you want me to ask my dad if he can get you another audition?'

'Nah,' I say. 'Thanks anyway, but they've got Captain Kickbutt all wrong. Their movie is not nearly funny enough for me. I'll find another way to get super famous. Maybe Duck and I can go on tour as a puppet show. What do they call them? Ventrilobots?'

'Ventriloquists,' Abby says. 'But would Duck be the puppet or you?'

'Oh, that's a good idea!' I say. 'He could stick his wing up my shirt and I could be the puppet. But wait, would that tickle?'

MAX, I WAS JOKING.

Duck and I had better start practising.

THE END

Are you ready for Funny Kid #7?
Look out for
FUNNY KID PEEKING DUCK!

This one is
PINK and Duck is
photobombing.

funny kid

You've read them all, right?

(1)

This one is BLUE and someone poops in the storeroom!

(2)

This one is RED and I get heckled by a clown!

(3)

This one is GREEN and I keep getting wet!

(4)

This one is ORANGE. You know, like an ... orange.

(5)

This one is PURPLE and I fall over a lot!

(6)

This one is as BLACK as half a zebra!

Thank you!

Making books is a team effort and I get to work with some of the best people!

So a huge thank you to Kate Burnitt, Chris Kunz, Shannon Kelly, Tegan Morrison, Kimberley Bennett, Cristina Cappelluto, Michelle Weisz, Chren Byng, Georgia Williams, Kady Holt, Jemma Myors, Alice Karsen, Kelli Lonergan, Fiona Luke, James Kellow, Amy Fox, Darren Kelly, Pauline O'Carolan, Brendon Redmond and Natalie Buckley-Cartwright. And to Beck, Bonnie, Boston and Miller – I adore you.

Books by Matt Stanton

Funny Kid series
Funny Kid for President
Funny Kid Stand Up
Funny Kid Prank Wars
Funny Kid Get Licked
Funny Kid Slapstick
Funny Kid Kicks Butt

Pea + Nut! picture books
Pea + Nut!

Fart Monster and Me series
with Tim Miller:
Fart Monster and Me: The Crash Landing
Fart Monster and Me: The New School
Fart Monster and Me: The Birthday Party
Fart Monster and Me: The Class Excursion

Fart Monster + Friends picture books
with Tim Miller:
There Is a Monster Under My Bed Who Farts
There Is a Monster Under My Christmas Tree Who Farts
There Is a Monster on My Holiday Who Farts
The Pirate Who Had to Pee
Dinosaur Dump
Don't Spew in Your Spacesuit
Burpzilla
Happy Farter's Day

Books That Drive Kids Crazy! picture books
with Beck Stanton:
This Is a Ball
Did You Take the B from My _ook?
The Red Book
Wait!
The Book That Never Ends

Matt Stanton is a bestselling children's author and illustrator, with over 850,000 books sold in Australia alone. He is the co-creator of the mega-hits *There Is a Monster Under My Bed Who Farts* and *This Is a Ball*. *Funny Kid for President* debuted as the #1 Australian kids' book and the Funny Kid series is fast winning legions of fans around the world.

mattstanton.net

Funny Kid Army!
Come and subscribe to Matt's YouTube Channel!

We learn to draw funny stuff!

Talk about how to write funny stories!

And sometimes we launch a book out of a cannon!

MattStantonTV
youtube.com/mattstanton